"Barbara ... me. I wa ...

Jock's statement roused Barbara's anger. "This isn't a game!" she protested. "You can't play tug-of-war with me!"

"Barbara's right," Todd sided with her. "She isn't mine to give back to you. It's her choice to make."

"Then you might as well give Todd his ring back right now," Jock instructed her.

"How typically arrogant of you!" she raged. "What makes you think I would prefer you?"

Jock brought himself within a foot of her. The powerful magnetic aura that surrounded him trapped Barbara in its force field as securely as if he'd taken her in his arms. His dangerous virility sent the adrenaline surging through her veins, heightening all her senses.

And she realized that she had the answer to her question....

JANET DAILEY AMERICANA

ALABAMA—Dangerous Masquerade
ALASKA—Northern Magic
ARIZONA—Sonora Sundown
ARKANSAS—Valley of the Vapours
CALIFORNIA—Fire and Ice
COLORADO—After the Storm
CONNECTICUT—Difficult Decision
DELAWARE—The Matchmakers
FLORIDA—Southern Nights
GEORGIA—Night of the Cotillion
HAWAII—Kona Winds
IDAHO—The Travelling Kind
ILLINOIS—A Lyon's Share
INDIANA—The Indy Man
IOWA—The Homeplace
KANSAS—The Mating Season
KENTUCKY—Bluegrass King
LOUISIANA—The Bride of the Delta Queen
MAINE—Summer Mahogany
MARYLAND—Bed of Grass
MASSACHUSETTS—That Boston Man
MICHIGAN—Enemy in Camp
MINNESOTA—Giant of Mesabi
MISSISSIPPI—A Tradition of Pride
MISSOURI—Show Me

MONTANA—Big Sky Country
NEBRASKA—Boss Man from Ogallala
NEVADA—Reilly's Woman
NEW HAMPSHIRE—Heart of Stone
NEW JERSEY—One of the Boys
NEW MEXICO—Land of Enchantment
NEW YORK—Beware of the Stranger
NORTH CAROLINA—That Carolina Summer
NORTH DAKOTA—Lord of the High Lonesome
OHIO—The Widow and the Wastrel
OKLAHOMA—Six White Horses
OREGON—To Tell the Truth
PENNSYLVANIA—The Thawing of Mara
RHODE ISLAND—Strange Bedfellow
SOUTH CAROLINA—Low Country Liar
SOUTH DAKOTA—Dakota Dreamin'
TENNESSEE—Sentimental Journey
TEXAS—Savage Land
UTAH—A Land Called Deseret
VERMONT—Green Mountain Man
VIRGINIA—Tide Water Lover
WASHINGTON—For Mike's Sake
WEST VIRGINIA—Wild and Wonderful
WISCONSIN—With a Little Luck
WYOMING—Darling Jenny

Janet Dailey
Americana

SOUTHERN NIGHTS

Harlequin Books

TORONTO • NEW YORK • LONDON
AMSTERDAM • PARIS • SYDNEY • HAMBURG
STOCKHOLM • ATHENS • TOKYO • MILAN

The state flower depicted on the cover of this book is
orange blossom.

Janet Dailey Americana edition published October 1986
Second printing May 1988
Third printing May 1989

ISBN 373-21909-1

Harlequin Presents edition published July 1980
Second printing February 1982

Original hardcover edition published in 1980
by Mills & Boon Limited

CHAPTER ONE

THE TRAFFIC HAD THINNED since Miami was left behind, enabling Todd Gaynor to relax behind the wheel. Barbara slid closer to him and he obligingly curved an arm around her shoulders to nestle her against his side. His hand affectionately rumpled the short curls of her black silk hair.

Taking his eyes from the highway long enough to glance at the head resting on his shoulder, he queried, ''Tired?''

''Mmm.'' It was a soft, negative sound. Through half-closed lashes Barbara saw the late-afternoon sunlight glinting off the waters of Lake Okeechobee.

''Nervous?'' Todd pressed a light kiss against her hair.

''A little,'' she admitted. It was difficult to be too nervous. Todd was her rock. With him she felt safe and protected, not dangling on the edge of a precipice about to take a nasty fall. His strength gave her the courage to face anything—even something as potentially daunting as meeting his family.

''In love?''

Just for a moment, the husky inflection of his voice made her heart flutter in reaction to the memory of another man's voice. Snuggling closer to Todd, Barbara forced the sensation to go away.

"Yes," she answered, perhaps too fervently in her attempt to deny the unwanted memory.

"I'm in love, too."

"Are you?" Enveloped in the warmth of his arm, it was easy for Barbara to match his light, bantering tone.

"Yes. With a beautiful woman ... with hair like black satin and hauntingly lovely blue eyes."

"I hope she makes you very happy." Her hand sought the arm around her shoulders to lace its fingers with his. It was a gesture oddly reminiscent of another time, and another man's hand entwined possessively with hers. A shudder trembled through her.

"Are you cold?" Todd was instantly attentive. "Shall I turn the air conditioner down?"

"No, I'm fine," she insisted, and tilted her head back against his arm to gaze at his face. "Sometimes it seems that I've known you all my life instead of one short month. Todd—" there was a catch in her voice, a poignant throb "—I wish I had met you first."

He slid her a look before letting his attention return to the highway. "Do you want to talk about him?" It was a gentle question that didn't probe but rather invited.

A pregnant silence followed his question. Barbara was barely aware of it as her gaze ran over the strong, handsome profile of his face that at times reminded her of Jock. So did a half a hundred other men whose facial bone structure was similar. But the likeness ended there. Todd's hair and eyes were brown, not gilded with gold. At thirty-one, he lacked the character lines that had etched Jock's eyes and mouth. Nor did he possess that potent brand of sexuality that had taken Barbara's breath away the first time she saw Jock on the beach. She had only to close her eyes to remember the hard feel of his body against hers and the undermining caress of his sure hands.

"What's there to talk about?" A bitter hurt that Barbara had thought was behind her crept into her voice. "He dropped me like a rock."

It was no good to claim that only her pride had suffered from the blow. Nor could she claim that he had taken advantage of her. She had gone into the affair with her eyes wide open, never dreaming it would last less than a week. For her, it had meant everything.

His huskily seductive voice echoed in her head, saying the words she'd heard six months before. "I'm not any good at small talk, honey. I want to make love to you." The forthright statement had not offended her. Jock Malloy had only been saying what had been on her mind whenever he was within touching distance.

"Did I tell you that he once asked me to go with him when he left?" It was a short, mocking question, filled with self-derision. She had thought many times about that offer, and also her reaction to it. She flashed Todd a brittle smile. "I nearly agreed. I was so tempted.... But I kept thinking about my job, and my apartment. Can you imagine the mess I would have been in if I had gone with him and he'd got tired of me and dumped me between here and Texas or wherever his ranch was—if he had one?''

Details hadn't mattered at the time. She had known Jock was vacationing in Miami, and the beach house where he was staying belonged to a friend. Stupidly, she had never considered it to be a holiday affair that would come to an abrupt end when he left. She was so positive it would continue that she had never bothered to ask questions about him. Talking had been the least of their interests. Jock's form of communication had been so much more satisfactory. Afterward Barbara was glad she didn't know any details about him other than his name and the vaguely mentioned fact that he had a cattle ranch.

''But you didn't go with him,'' Todd pointed out, his arm tightening around her.

''No.'' A sudden, vaguely desperate sigh broke from her. ''Why am I telling you all this?''

''Confession is supposed to be good for the soul.'' He grinned down at her.

''I . . . can't.'' She moved compulsively out of his arms to the passenger side of the luxury sedan. Other than the bare bones of her story, Barbara had never fleshed out the affair to Todd. Even now he wasn't asking her to, only offering a willing ear to listen. Her refusal to confide in him didn't produce a reaction. Tapping out a cigarette from her pack, Barbara lighted it and blew out an impatient stream of smoke. ''Why haven't you ever asked about him, Todd? His name? How we met? What happened?'' Her sideways glance was wary, apprehension shimmering in the blue depths of her eyes.

"Because I know that someday you'll trust me enough to tell me the whole story," he answered without hesitation.

"I do trust you." Barbara glanced at the diamond solitaire glittering on her left hand. The engagement ring was indicative of her trust. She had promised to place her heart in his keeping. It had been shattered when she met Todd, but he had made her heart whole again. He had given her so much that she wasn't certain how much she could return. "Doesn't it bother you that there was someone else before you came?"

"No. A woman doesn't reach the age of twenty-five without her heart getting bruised and battered along the way. I accepted that when I met you." He reached across the seat to hold her hand.

Barbara studied the gentle strength of his fingers warmly clasping hers. Their touch didn't make her skin tingle, but she didn't trust that sensation anymore. His comment prompted a fleeting curiosity to voice itself.

"What about your heart? Has it ever been bruised and battered, Todd?" She found it hard to believe. His face was so smooth and calm, bearing no scars of tormented longing and heartbroken grief.

"A half a dozen times, at least." It came out like a joke.

"Be serious," Barbara insisted.

"I am. It's difficult to judge past emotional involvements since I have met you. From this perspective, they all seem like infatuations. Does that answer your question?'' He briefly arched an eyebrow in her direction, his brown eyes warm with amused indulgence.

''Yes, I suppose it does.'' She hadn't yet gained that perspective for herself to be sure.

''Besides, if you had met me first, maybe you wouldn't have noticed me,'' Todd suggested with a teasing wink.

''That isn't true,'' Barbara protested quickly. ''You are a very handsome man, Todd Gaynor. Any woman would notice you.'' Unless Jock Malloy was around, a hateful little voice qualified her statement.

As if reading her mind, Todd followed his thought one step further. ''Or maybe I would have lost you to him.'' Barbara was thankful he didn't give her a chance to respond to that remark, because she didn't know what she could say to that distinct possibility. ''The 'maybes' don't have anything to do with the present or the way it happened. There isn't any reason to say 'what if?' ''

''Yes, there is,'' she said in a sober voice. ''What if I had never met you? You have been so good *to* me and *for* me, and *with* me—'' she emphasized the prepositions ''—that sometimes I wonder what I did to deserve someone like you who is so understanding and patient.''

''When I first met you, you reminded me of a stray kitten I once found that someone had dumped on the highway,'' Todd mused. ''You were so scared and frightened . . . not that you let it show.'' He darted her an amused glance. ''No, you arched your back and hissed at me, pretending you weren't scared or frightened just as that little black kitten did. How many times did you turn me down before I finally persuaded you to come out with me?''

''At least twelve.'' Barbara remembered his gentle persistence in coaxing her out of the reclusive shell she had hidden in. ''Although I don't know why you bothered,'' she sighed.

Letting go of her hand, Todd reached up and flipped down the sun visor on her side. The mirror on the back side of the visor reflected her image, midnight black hair framing an oval face, brilliant blue eyes outlined by long, sooty lashes, a stunning combination of features that were enhanced by a golden Florida tan.

''That woman in the mirror should answer your questions,'' he said. ''When I first met her, there were dark circles under her eyes and a lovely mouth that had forgotten how to smile or laugh. Look what love has done.''

A passing thought crossed her mind that love had made the dark circles and smileless mouth in the first place. Barbara didn't mention it, but she couldn't keep the pain of remembering that shattering anguish of lost love from flickering across her expression.

''I promised I wouldn't rush you into marriage, Barbara, and I won't. We'll have a long engagement, an old-fashioned courtship period where I can shower you with presents and flowers and love poems.'' A bantering note in his voice seemed to tease his own romanticism and make her smile with him. ''It will all culminate in a big church wedding, which will make my mother happy, and a Caribbean honeymoon, which will make me happy. You'll like my mother,'' he added unexpectedly.

"I hope she'll like me,'' was the automatic response.

"She will,'' Todd assured her. "I wish we'd had more time together for ourselves. I wouldn't have suggested spending our vacations with my family if either one of us could arrange to take them later this year. But these two weeks are the only slack time the hotel has before the Easter crunch hits, then summer tourists. My manager takes his vacation in the fall and—''

"The airline wouldn't let me rearrange my schedule unless I gave up my vacation for this year,'' Barbara inserted. She worked the reservation counter at the airport, after flying the first two years as a stewardess with the same company. "It is sheer coincidence that we have the same vacation time now.''

"I know,'' he smiled. "And I want you to get to know my family. I want you to think of them as yours.''

"You haven't told me very much about your family. There is your mother who is a widow, and your brother,'' she began, and Todd picked up the conversation from that point.

"There are just my mother and brother, but we have always been very close. Maybe because there are just the three of us. My mother, Lillian, is a great lady. Gentle, warm and loving.''

"You must take after her,'' Barbara concluded.

"I don't know. My dad was a pretty great guy, too. Mom said he was the softest touch in town. When any charity in Miami needed to raise money, they stopped at his hotel first. He couldn't say no to anyone in trouble. If he had, he'd probably have been a multimillionaire when he died. Not that he left us broke!" Todd laughed at the thought.

Only in the last few weeks had Barbara begun to realize that she was engaged to a relatively wealthy man. The hotel Todd owned and operated was one of the plushest resorts on the oceanfront strip. The income from it could have enabled him to enjoy the role of playboy, but Todd had chosen to work.

"What about Sandoval?" she asked, referring to the citrus farm that was their destination. "Is that where you grew up?"

"No. We did spend time there. J.R. liked it but I'm not much of a country boy. I prefer city life, like my dad," Todd admitted.

Looking at him, Barbara was glad. She preferred his casual refinement to the leathered look of an outdoorsman. It would have been an unwanted reminder of a man browned to a teak color from hours in the sun. Like her's, Todd's suntan came from lazing by a pool or on an ocean beach.

"J.R. is your brother?" she asked for confirmation.

"My older brother, yes. It's a good thing Sandoval belongs to him. That life fits him like a glove. I should warn you about J.R.," Todd added after a second's consideration.

"Warn me?" Her blue eyes sent him a quizzical

glance as a little shiver of fear danced down her spine.

Todd met her look with a silently laughing smile. "He's going to make a pass at you."

"But why? I mean . . . I'm your fiancée. Surely he wouldn't—" She tried to stammer out an astonished protest, but Todd laughed out loud.

"In the first place, J.R. has a roving eye that invariably locates a beautiful woman in a crowd," he began his explanation. "Plus he has always held a fatal fascination for the opposite sex. Which was something he discovered early on. Knowing J.R., any advances he might make toward you would have a twofold purpose. One would be to test you—to see if the woman engaged to his brother is really sincere."

"And the second?" Barbara prompted when Todd paused.

"The second reason?" He lifted his shoulders in an expressive shrug. "The second reason would probably be for the sheer hell of it."

"What am I supposed to do when he makes this pass?" She couldn't keep the edge of challenge out of her voice.

"I can't tell you what to do." There was an underlying chuckle in his voice. "All I can do is warn you in advance that it's coming. I trust you to know how to handle him, Barbara."

Slightly reassured by his confidence in her, she commented on a cynical note, "I take it your brother isn't married?"

"J.R. is the original swamp fox, too wily and

experienced to be caught in the marriage trap. His problem is he's always had the pick of the bunch. Anything that was out of his reach, he regarded as sour grapes. Actually, I think as far as the female sex is concerned J.R. could take them or leave them. Mostly he takes them, then leaves them.'' Todd grinned at his description.

But Barbara was mulling over his first statement. ''Todd, do you regard marriage as a trap?''

The smile was wiped from his well-defined mouth. ''No. I was being facetious, repeating attitudes that are usually attributed to my brother. They aren't really fair to him. I think he would like to have a wife and children, if he could ever find the right girl. He needs someone like you, Barbara, that he can protect and cherish.'' His arm curved around her shoulders again to draw her to his side. ''J.R. has just had too many eager applicants for the position. He tends to view them all with a jaundiced eye.''

''You really care a lot about your brother, don't you?'' Barbara realized with a vague sense of shock. From Todd's description, the two seemed to be such opposites.

''I have hero-worshipped him for too many years. He may have feet of clay, but J.R. is still someone to look up to,'' Todd insisted. ''You'll know what I mean when you meet him.''

She relaxed in his arms. There was no reason to disbelieve what he said. If his brother was half as nice as Todd was, Barbara knew she would like him.

''What have you told your family about me?'' she asked curiously.

"Nothing."

"Nothing?" She sat up straighter and turned to look at him.

A lazy smile tugged at the corners of his mouth. "Knowing my mother, if I told her I was bringing my future bride home with me, she'd have everyone at the place come to the house for a champagne party. I don't think you are prepared for that kind of a welcome. It's too soon for us yet. So I just told her I was bringing a friend with me. That way you can have a few quiet days to get acquainted before she throws the inevitable engagement party." He slowed the car and turned off the highway onto a narrow lane where he stopped in front of a gate. "We are now on Sandoval land."

Barbara glanced at the plain wooden gate painted white. A small sign on the top rail stated: Sandoval Ranch—Private Property—No Trespassing.

"That isn't very welcoming," she remarked of the sign.

"The main entrance is a few miles up the road yet," Todd explained. "This is a shortcut to the house, as well as a scenic drive through the orchards. Wait here while I open the gate." He switched off the air conditioner and rolled down the car windows before climbing out of the car to open the gate.

The tangy fragrance of oranges drifted on the warm air that filled the artificially cooled interior of the car. Precise, orderly rows of dwarf trees flanked the narrow dirt road beyond the gate Todd opened. As he drove the car through and stopped to close the gate, Barbara had a closer look at the deep orange balls of fruit hanging from the tree limbs.

"Valencia," Todd identified the variety. "There are probably more Valencia orange groves on the property than any other. Their flavor makes them excellent juice oranges. My mother uses them in fruit salads and dessert cups. They start to ripen in March so they will be picking these soon."

"For a city boy, you seem very knowledgeable about oranges," Barbara teased.

"Isn't every Floridian supposed to be an expert on oranges?" he countered.

"Not this one," she admitted. "I've driven past a lot of orange groves and stopped at fruit stands to buy the native product, but what I know about citrus fruit wouldn't fill a page."

Todd drove slowly along the narrow lane. "We'll try to correct that while you are here."

"Look." Barbara pointed at the tree on the driver's side. "Isn't that an orange blossom on the same limb where there is an orange?"

"Yes. You are about to receive your first lecture on citrus fruit. Oranges and grapefruit take a full twelve months to mature, unlike apples and other fruit that mature in three or four months. Therefore, you have ripened fruit and blossoms on the tree at the same time—this year's crop and next year's."

After seeing the first blossom, Barbara spotted more white petals sprinkled through the green leaves of the trees and contrasting with the orange globes of fruit. The car rolled slowly past the arrow-straight rows of trees that seemed to stretch endlessly.

"Oranges and grapefruit won't ripen once they are picked like other fruit. So they can't be picked when they are green and shipped to the cities. They have to be tree ripened," Todd explained.

"I didn't know that, either." Barbara laughed at her own ignorance.

"Tomorrow I'll arrange to take you on a complete tour of the citrus groves and make up for your neglected education. How would you like that?"

"I'd love it."

As they rounded a turn, the groves of fruit trees were replaced by hayfields. Ahead Barbara could see white rail fences and green grass beyond the purple blossoms of clover. In the lush pastures, sunlight glistened on the sleekly coated hides of grazing horses. A spindly-legged foal stood next to its mother close to the fence.

"You raise horses?" Barbara asked in surprise.

"Mm, thoroughbreds for racing. Didn't I mention that?"

"No, you didn't mention it," she returned with amusement, and looked again to the pastures. "Aren't they beautiful?"

"Do you ride?"

"Every chance I get—which isn't many." A wistful note crept into her voice.

"There are more than enough horses here. You can ride a different one every day if you want," Todd offered.

"This place is beginning to sound like paradise."

"We are going to be marooned here for two weeks," Todd said.

"I'm not going to mind." The roofs of the stables were coming into sight, white gleaming buildings to match the white rail fences.

"I'm not going to mind, either, not when I'm spending these two weeks with you. I'll probably be so busy looking at you that I won't even miss the bright lights," he concluded, warming her with a look that made her feel loved.

Irrespective of the fact that he was driving, Barbara leaned to kiss him. It was a spontaneous gesture, the first kiss she had initiated between them. Once she had been much bolder, but then it had been another man's mouth she sought.

Todd let the car slow to a crawl as his mouth moved in instant response to her kiss. She liked the feel of his lips tasting hers, their gentle persuasion that sent such a contented glow flowing through her veins. He promised a different kind of satisfaction, one less dangerous and soul-destroying.

"I love you," she whispered, her lips feathering the outline of his mouth.

He seemed to hesitate. Then the arm that had held her close pushed her shoulders against the seat back, setting her away from him. The ardent light in his brown eyes said her declaration had disturbed him, but common sense had taken control.

"Then you'd better let me see where I'm going before we run into something," he suggested.

"You are right," she conceded and settled comfortably against his shoulder, contented with the pleasant feeling the embrace had produced inside.

Todd chuckled and drew her glance. "Why are you laughing?"

"You look like a kitten with a faceful of cream."

"I am happy," Barbara admitted to being that smugly satisfied. "I never thought I would be again."

He seemed to know that no reply was expected from him, although his hand tightened on her arm in silent understanding. From the tree-shaded pastures of green grass, past the white boards of the stables, the narrow lane led toward an oak-studded lawn. Rising in the midst of the treetops was a red-tiled roof. The narrow lane connected with the black asphalt of the main road to the house.

As Todd turned onto the main road, the Spanish moss draped from the branches kept the house from view. Her eyes widened when the gray green curtain was lifted. A massive two-story home rose in front of her, the dull red tile of the roof complimented by the natural color of the stucco walls. The dramatic arches and balconies spoke of the traditional Spanish design. Arched exterior walls led into a courtyard with a dancing silver fountain, and more arches led to the main entrance. Black wrought iron, scrolled like lace, lined the balconies on the upper floor, covered by arched frames.

"Are you going to sit in the car and admire, or should we go inside?" Todd chided.

Overwhelmed by the magnificence of the house, Barbara hadn't realized Todd had stopped the car and turned off the engine. She gave a guilty start of surprise at his question.

"You should have warned me it was so impressive," she said in quick recovery.

"I think I had probably forgotten until I saw it through your eyes," he admitted and climbed out of the car to walk around and open her door. "But it's just a house, Barbara. Four walls and a roof."

It was more than four walls and a roof, but Barbara didn't argue the point. For all its old-world grandeur, the house didn't intimidate. A riot of bougainvillea crowded the walls of the courtyard where the water playing in the fountain made a happy sound. The noise of their footsteps on the tiled walkway didn't seem an intrusion as they entered the courtyard. More greenery hung from macrame-suspended pots while a profusion of blossoms colored stone urns. Beyond another archway, Barbara saw the blue waters of a swimming pool. But it was to the huge carved doors that Todd guided her.

The door opened into a tiled foyer. A second, glass-doored entrance into the foyer came from the porch on the pool side of the house. The carved balustrade of an open staircase curved gracefully from the foyer to the second floor. A glazed archway opened into the living room. Todd paused inside this spacious room.

"Would you mind waiting here?" he asked. "Mother is probably in the kitchen and I don't think she would thank me if I took you back there when she might be having a row with the cook."

"I don't mind waiting here." Since Todd hadn't told his mother he was bringing his fiancée, the announcement might come as a shock. Barbara thought it was better is she wasn't around when Mrs. Gaynor was informed of their engagement.

"Are you thirsty? I'll bring us back something to drink if you are," he offered.

"I'd like that," she nodded.

He started toward the archway into the dining room with its heavy Spanish-designed furniture, then stopped and came back to kiss her lightly on the mouth. "Don't go running off. Mother will love you."

Strangely, Barbara discovered she didn't feel nervous about meeting his mother. Maybe the warm, comfortable atmosphere of the house had reassured her somehow. She glanced around the spacious living room with its white walls, arched windows and fireplace. It could have been so stiffly formal. Instead the cheery rugs on the tiled floor and the abundant pillows on the sofa took away from the rigidity of the Spanish furniture. The impression was one of solidity and relaxed comfort.

CHAPTER TWO

A DOOR SLAMMED in the foyer, glass rattling in the pane to indicate the pool-side entrance. Barbara turned toward the archway at the sound of long striding boots on the tiled floor. A tall, broad-shouldered man entered the living room, faded denims hugging narrow hips and muscled thighs. The dusty and perspiration-stained shirt had once been white, just as the wide-brimmed Stetson on the man's head had once been brown. The shadowing brim of that hat hid his features until some unconscious movement from Barbara betrayed her presence and the head came up.

A shock wave trembled through her bones at the sight of the hard, male features toughened by the sun. A pair of tawny eyes flicked over her like twin tongues of lightning. Her imagination was playing some cruel trick on her. It had to be, she insisted frantically. The hat came off, sailed by a hand to land on a chair. Brown hair was streaked with gold, the handiwork of the sun. The action was followed by the white flash of a smile, virile features etched with stunning sexuality.

"Jock." The name was wrenched from the stranglehold of disbelief that gripped her throat.

"You changed your mind and decided to accept my invitation after all." That low, drawling voice ran over her like a caress. "It took you long enough."

It was a dream. Barbara was convinced it had to be. It was a mirage coming toward her. Jock's only invitation had been to come with him. Later he had let her know it was all over between them. So he wouldn't be saying something like that.

But it was no mirage that swept her into his arms and crushed her slender frame to the hard contours of his body. The weight of his mouth on hers forced her head back while he kissed her with a hungry, pillaging force that was destructive and passionate. Her fingers were splayed across his shoulders, feeling the ripple of flexing muscles through the damp, thin cotton of his shirt.

The hard dominance of his embrace pierced her numbed senses to send them reeling with a dangerous excitement. The wildly violent emotion quaking through her was undermining defenses Barbara had vowed would never be breached again. Yet the deliberate mastery of his kiss was crumbling her resistance as if its walls were wafer thin. That abandoned hunger within was aiding in the destruction. The searing, molding prowess of his hands was awakening her flesh to his desires and making them her own. Confusion reigned in what little coherent thought that remained. When his mouth trailed down her throat to explore the pulsing hollow of her shoulder, Barbara fought through the haze of wild sensation.

"What are you doing here, Jock?" Her voice

wavered in traitorous betrayal of the havoc he was wreaking on her control.

"What the hell kind of question is that?" The warmth of his laughing breath caressed her sensitive skin. He lifted his head long enough to let the gold shock of his eyes hold her victim. Then his mouth came down near her lips, his breath mingling with hers as he answered amusedly, "I live here, of course."

And the hot languor of his kiss was consuming her again, carrying her to a high precipice where the view was heady and the height was terrifying. The dizzying heights hadn't frightened her before, but that was before Barbara had fallen into the deep abyss below. Todd had forced her out of that black pit of depression. It was his voice that penetrated the drugging rapture that held her captive now.

"Mother sent me out with the drinks. She'll—" His voice stopped in midsentence.

The muscled chest beneath Barbara's hands expanded in a deep breath of control as Jock lifted his mouth from its possession of hers and sent an impatient glance beyond her. The gold-flecked eyes returned quickly to her face, roaming her passion-dazed features with lazy pleasure.

"Your timing is off, little brother," Jock criticized on an indolent note, never letting his gaze stray from her upturned face. "Go away and arrange to arrive about an hour from now. Better make it two hours," he corrected adding softly to Barbara, "It's been a long time and I may not be so quickly satisfied."

His arrogant presumption that she would gladly return to him despite the fact that he had thrown her aside in the past was the spark her pride needed. Todd's presence in the room and the engagement ring on her finger gave Barbara the strength to retaliate. In one motion, she pushed out of his arms and struck. The palm of her hand connected with stinging force against a leanly hollowed cheek. His stunned look was immediately replaced with yellow fury, hard and glittering when it focused on her. Sensing she had roused a wild beast, Barbara cautiously began to back toward Todd.

His low laughter split the air fraught with a dangerours tension. "I told you that you would know how to handle J.R. when the time came." The firm clasp of his hand was on her shoulder. Barbara turned into it, seeking the protection and safety of Todd's nearness. "Although I have to admit I didn't expect the time to come so soon, and judging by the look on your face, J.R., I don't think you expected so violent a rebuff."

Barbara risked a glance at Jock. A hand was rubbing his cheek where she had slapped him. There was a wary glitter in his eyes, as if he was trying to assess this puzzling situation, too. She didn't understand why Todd kept calling him J.R. How could Jock be his brother?

"Should I bother with formal introductions?" Todd was still finding amusement in the situation. "Or are you just going to congratulate me for finding such a beautiful fiancée?"

"The two of you are engaged?" If Todd didn't

hear the deadly quiet note in Jock's voice, Barbara did.

"Didn't you show him your ring, Barbara?" Todd's voice prompted her to correct the omission.

"I didn't have the chance." Which was the truth. Her left hand was stiffly resistant to the orders sent along her motor nerves. At last it was lifted to display the diamond solitaire on her ring finger to the piercing gold gaze that examined it.

"This all happened a little suddenly, didn't it, Todd?" There was a measure of challenge in Jock's seemingly idle comment.

"We only met a month ago," Todd admitted and smiled at Barbara, not apparently noticing her brittle expression. "But I copied a page from your book, J.R., and didn't waste any time once I found her."

"I don't understand," Barbara finally voiced her troubled confusion. "You two are brothers, yet with different—"

"Half brothers," Jock interrupted. "Same mother, different fathers. Didn't Todd mention that?" The edges of his mouth curved up, a lazy smile that mocked her ignorance. It also relayed his discovery that he now realized she had no previous knowledge that she would find him here.

"No, he didn't mention that," she admitted flatly, sickened by the situation she was trapped in.

"Todd is the only one who calls me J.R. To everyone else I'm Jock."

"Jock Malloy." Barbara didn't know why she said his whole name unless it was to beat it into her brain. A wasted effort since it was already branded in her memory.

What was more, it was perfectly obvious that she hadn't identified him to Todd as the man with whom she'd had that disastrous affair. She knew it. And Jock knew it. Poor Todd was the only one who didn't. How long could she keep it a secret from Todd? How long before Jock told him? Would he try to blackmail her with the knowledge? And to what end?

"You look pale, Barbara," Jock observed, a faint gleam of satisfaction in his wolf-gold eyes. "May I call you Barbara?" He taunted her with their secret knowledge that he had called her many other things when they had made love six months before. "Aren't you feeling well?"

"I . . . ." She swallowed at the lump choking her throat. "I do have a headache." A terrible, throbbing one that clawed at her temples. "Probably from the trip," she lied. "I used to get carsick as a child."

"Why don't you sit down, Barbara?" Todd suggested and attentively guided her to the sofa and its many plump pillows. As she sat down, his hand happened to rest on the tension-strained muscles of her neck. "You are tense . . . all strung out like a wire."

"Nerves, I guess." Under the scrutiny of Jock's tawny eyes, Barbara knew she would never relax, but for Todd's sake she tried to appear that way.

"She needs a rubdown, Todd. A good massage would work wonders for tense muscles." Jock's look was deliberately suggestive of other, more intimate times despite the bland tone he used.

"You've always been better at that sort of thing than I will ever be." Indirectly Todd gave his permission.

Barbara instantly protested when Jock took a step toward the couch where she sat. "No!" She tempered the explosive refusal with a more even explanation. "It really isn't necessary. An aspirin would work just as well."

"Todd, why don't you get her one from the medicine cabinet?" suggested Jock.

"I have some in my purse." Barbara blocked that attempt to get her alone again. She would have to face him alone sooner or later, but not yet. Not until she mastered some immunity to him. Just having his eyes on her reminded Barbara of sensations she would rather forget.

When Jock handed the straw purse to her, Barbara only had to see his hands to remember how expertly they aroused her and how intimately they knew her.

"Thank you." She offered him the polite phrase and lifted her gaze to his face.

The clean, decisive outline of his mouth arrested her attention. Its latent sensuality forced vivid recollections of the explorations of that mouth to discover all the special places that stimulated her excitement. Heat flamed her skin as Barbara hurriedly bent her head to look for the bottle of aspirin in her purse.

"Can't you find what you are looking for?" Jock mocked.

A hole to crawl into and hide was what she wanted, but it was an aspirin bottle she found. Prying off the safety cap, she took out two tablets in her palm. Todd was offering her a tall, iced glass.

"Mother fixed some orange concoction. Would you prefer water?" he asked.

"No, this is fine." She washed down the tablets with the fresh citrus drink. "Where is your mother?" In a nervous gesture, Barbara raked her fingernails through the dark curls near her ear, ostensibly fluffing her hair, and reached for her purse again.

"She wanted a few minutes to freshen up before she met you," Todd explained.

A lighted cigarette was extended to her, filtered end first, just as Barbara found her own pack of cigarettes in her purse. She didn't need to look to know whose hand owned those strong, sun-browned fingers, so capable and adept at lovemaking.

"It will help calm your nerves," Jock murmured.

"I have some of my own, thank you," Barbara attempted a refusal, not able to keep out that taut breathlessness in her voice.

"It's the same brand." The inflection added a silent and mocking "remember?" to cause that rush of heat in her ckeeks to color her again.

"Thank you." She took the cigarette from his fingers. Her imagination helped to increase the warm taste of his mouth on the filtered tip. As her lips absorbed the flavor of his, her darkened blue eyes made a furtive glance at his teak-hard face, ricocheting away when she found his gaze centered on her mouth. The click of heels on the tiled floor heralded the arrival of Todd's mother and gave Barbara an excellent excuse to crush the cigarette in the ashtray.

"I'm sorry I took so long, but Todd caught me unaware." A tall, handsome woman entered the living room, her dark hair liberally streaked with gray. Her warm smile and all her attention were directed strictly at Barbara. Alert brown eyes swept her in silent appraisal. Apparently she was dissatisfied with the result. ''When Todd mentioned he was bringing a friend, I thought. . . . It doesn't matter what I thought.''

Barbara rose from the sofa automatically at the woman's approach, with Todd standing at her side. But it was Jock, leaning back in his chair, so relaxed, with lazy amusement gleaming in his eyes, who made the introduction.

''Mother, meet your future daughter-in-law, Barbara Haynes.''

''How do you do, Mrs. Gaynor.'' Her greeting sounded stiff, so stiff when in fact the woman was so like Todd that Barbara wanted to cry with relief.

''Lillian, please,'' the woman corrected, putting them on a first-name basis immediately. ''And I'll call you Barbara. Welcome to Sandoval.''

''Thank you. It's good of you to have me.''

Brown eyes sparkled in the look they darted to Todd. ''She's very beautiful.''

''Don't sound so surprised, mother.'' He laughed and slid a hand around Barbara's waist.

''You'll have to forgive me, Barbara, if I am at a loss for words. This engagement has come as such a surprise. Todd hasn't even mentioned you so I didn't have any inkling that he was serious about anyone.'' Realizing that she was making everyone stand because of her, Lillian Gaynor insisted, ''Please, sit down.'' She took a chair close to the sofa. ''How long have you known each other? How did you meet?''

''We bumped into each other a month ago, literally,'' Todd answered, draping an arm along the sofa back behind Barbara. ''She walked into my car at the airport as I was backing out of a parking space.''

''Were you hurt?'' was Lillian's instant concern.

''No.''

''I took one look at her and insisted that I had to see her home safely,'' Todd said with a wink. ''After considerable arguing and persuading I finally convinced her to go out with me. She didn't have a very high opinion of men at the time or—''

Barbara felt a pair of gold brown eyes narrow on her and quickly interrupted ''Todd,'' she cautioned. She had escaped the affair with Jock with a few scattered remnants of her pride intact. She didn't want Todd unintentionally taking that away from her.

Todd hesitated, then smiled. ''—or it wouldn't have taken me so long.'' He changed what he had been about to say.

''May I see your ring?'' Lillian asked and Barbara showed her the diamond Todd had given her. ''It's a beautiful stone. When is the wedding? Have you set a date?''

''Not yet. Give us time, mother,'' Todd chided affectionately. ''We've been talking about a long engagement and a big wedding.''

''I don't suppose there is any need to rush, not in this day and age.'' Nobody misinterpreted Jock's innuendo. While Barbara reddened under his knowing regard, Todd flashed him a silencing look.

It was Lillian who reprimanded him. "Instead of being so cynical, Jock, you should be following Todd's example."

"I would," he stated. "But I don't think Todd would share his bride with me."

A wild sensation quivered in the pit of Barbara's stomach, a direct reaction to his suggestion. His eyes reminded her of the polished brilliance of the tigereye gemstones, a rich brown shot with gold. Jock was too rawly masculine and she was trapped in the magnetic field of his virile dominance, powerless to deny the compelling excitement he generated within her while mentally resisting his attraction.

"Too right I wouldn't share her," Todd declared, taking Jock's remark as a joke.

"Too right?" A quizzical brow was lifted in the hard lean face. "What did you have—a convention of Australians at the hotel?"

"A charter group," Todd admitted with a chuckle. "They all checked out this morning."

Todd may have missed the electric undercurrents sizzling in the air between Jock and Barbara, but Lillian Gaynor didn't. She sent Barbara a troubled look, sensing how much her oldest son's presence unnerved her without knowing why.

"Jock, don't you think you should shower and change?" Lillian suggested.

Jock appeared unconcerned by his sweaty and dusty appearance. Oddly, it only heightened that rough, manly aura that emanated from him. But he dutifully rose and retrieved his Stetson from the chair.

"I'll see you later," he said in parting, and Barbara had the distinct impression the supposed encompassing remark was meant for her.

Coming from the open stairwell, she heard the firm, hard clump of his work-scruffed boots on the steps, deliberate and unhurried. Barbara knew she was being granted only a temporary respite from his company, not nearly enough time to find a safe course out of this tangled situation.

"Did Todd offer you the cold drinks I fixed?" Lillian asked, then noticed the frosted glass on the side table near Barbara. "I see that he did."

"It's delicious." Barbara picked up the glass to sip the frosty cold mixture. "What's in it?"

"Fresh orange juice, egg and honey. It tastes much better than the ingredients sound," the woman laughed, but the conversation had been successfully diverted to a lighter vein of domesticity. After several minutes it naturally progressed to the suggestion by Lillian, "Let me show you which room you will have, Barbara. I imagine you will want to unpack and freshen up before dinner."

"Yes, I would. Thank you," she agreed quickly, grabbing at the offer to be alone even for a short time.

"I saw Arthur outside a few minutes ago, watering the flowers. He can help you with the luggage, Todd."

"All right."

While Todd exited the house through the heavy cypress doors, Barbara followed Lillian Gaynor up the open staircase to the second floor. Gleaming teakwood floors were a rich contrast to the continuation of white textured walls. The carved balustrade

protectively encircled the open stairwell, marking
the boundaries of the wide hall. All the bedrooms
opened onto the hall. Barbara's first thought was
which bedroom belonged to Jock, insisting to herself
that it was only self-defense that made her wonder.

"I think you'll like this room," Lillian was saying
as she walked to a carved, hardwood door to the right
of the three-tiered staircase. "It is reserved for special guests since it boasts a private bath and a private balcony. You are definitely a special guest,
Barbara."

"Unique" would have been a more fitting description, Barbara thought with irony. She doubted
that Lillian Gaynor would be quite so welcoming if
she knew she'd had an affair with one of her sons and
was engaged to marry the other.

The room was a stunning combination of turquoise and white with the dark wood of the furniture
for contrast. It was sparsely furnished since too
much of the heavy Mediterranean furniture would
weigh the room down and take away from its natural
spaciousness. A velvet spread of deep turquoise blue
covered the large, postered bed with its carved head-
board. The same turquoise color was repeated in the
Persian rug on the teakwood floor, and again in the
upholstery of the love seat. A double set of doors
opened into a huge closet and a second door led to a
mosaic-tiled bath with ornate Moorish fixtures.
Beyond glass-paned doors was the private balcony,
complete with black wrought-iron furniture spilling
over with brightly flowered blue cushions.

"It's lovely," Barbara admitted.

"I'm glad you like it." The sound of footsteps on

the stairs turned Lillian toward the door. "Here is Todd with your luggage. I'll leave you to unpack."

As she left the room, Todd walked in, juggling Barbara's three suitcases. "Where do you want them?"

"Just set them by the bed."

When his hands were free, he came back to put them around her. "How do you like my mom?"

"She's so much like you how could I help but love her?" Barbara admitted, sliding her fingers along the lapel of his summer jacket, and watching them instead of looking into Todd's face.

Sensing an aloofness that was emotional if not precisely physical, Todd curved a hand under her chin and lifted it. A concerned frown was in his expression.

"What's the matter, Barbara? Is something wrong?"

"No. Nothing," she insisted, but she couldn't keep the coolness out of her answer. She simply couldn't be comfortable in Todd's embrace, not when he didn't know about Jock.

"Is it J.R.?" Todd could so easily read her thoughts. "You aren't still upset about that pass he made, are you? You shouldn't let him bother you."

"Why indeed should I bother you?" Jock's mocking voice came from the doorway, causing Barbara to pivot out of Todd's arms with a guilty start. His tawny eyes were laughing at her, because he knew exactly why he bothered her. He was leaning indolently against the frame, his arms crossed in front of him. The faded denims and dirty shirt were gone, replaced by a silk shirt of pale yellow, open at the throat, and desert-brown pants. His appearance sensuously crisp and vital.

"So this is the room mother gave you." His gaze swept the room somewhat curiously, as if it had been a long time since he'd been inside it. "A nice big double bed." His gaze lingered on it before sliding to Barbara. "More than big enough for two."

"Come on, J.R. Barbara isn't that kind of girl," Todd defended her, but without anger or indignation.

"Isn't she?" Jock spoke as though he was surprised.

"No, she isn't." A troubled light entered Todd's brown eyes, indicating confusion at his brother's continued taunting.

"Stop it, Todd." The words rushed out in the low breath she exhaled. "I'm not a saint."

"You aren't a sinner, either." Now he was frowning at her.

"Must make you a martyr, Barbara," Jock declared with a twisted smile. Unfolding his arms, he straightened from the door frame. "Dinner is at seven. Sundowners on the veranda anytime before that. Come down whenever you're ready."

It was the first time Barbara had heard that crisp authority in his voice. It came very naturally. She realized Jock could command as well as seduce. She had known him only as a lover, and knew very little about him as a man.

"That doesn't give us much time, does it?" Todd murmured in a half sigh.

"No." Although she didn't have any idea what time it was.

"I'll stop by to see if you are ready before I go down," he promised and kissed her lightly on the cheek before he left the room.

It was an hour later before Todd knocked on her door. In that time Barbara had unpacked, showered and put on a blue-flowered dress. The soft material fell in natural folds that draped the scooped neckline and slimly fit the bodice and waist to flare in a skirt that swirled around her legs. Todd complimented her appearance, but Barbara couldn't take any pleasure in his approval. Together they made their way down the stairs and out onto the covered veranda at the pool side.

"Are you all settled in?" Lillian rose from a white wrought-iron chair to greet them, but Jock barely glanced their way from his position by the drink cart.

"Yes, thank you," Barbara nodded.

"If you are acting as bartender, J.R., I'll have a Scotch," Todd ordered.

"It's being splashed on ice right now." Jock tipped the bottle of liquor to pour it over the ice cubes in a squat glass. "What about you, Barbara? Something innocuous or would you rather get stoned with me?"

"Jock." Lillian admonished his cynical tone.

"Rum and Coke, please," Barbara ordered.

"I have to apologize for my son," Lillian stated somewhat ruefully. "Jock has been hard to get along with lately. He's been very moody these last few months."

"Some people claim there is a woman to blame,"
Jock stated, passing out their drinks. "Rum and
Coke. Scotch for you, Todd."

"A woman?" Todd jested. "More than likely,
it's women—in the plural."

Through the concealment of her lashes, Barbara
darted Jock a puzzled glance. Two phrases kept
echoing in her mind "moody these last few months"
... "a woman to blame." Was he trying to insinuate
that she'd had some sort of an aftereffect on him? It
was a heady thought, but she wouldn't permit it to
take root.

"To the future bride and groom." Lillian lifted
her glass in a toast to Todd and Barbara.

As the three sipped their drinks, Barbara noticed
that Jock didn't take part in the toast. His cocktail
glass was still sitting on the drink cart, conveniently
out of reach. He took his time returning to claim it.
Even then, he remained apart from them, aloof from
the small family celebration of their engagement,
and silent. His silence made Barbara equally uncomfortable as his taunting remarks had earlier. His
silence, and those watchful eyes....

CHAPTER THREE

THE COOK, a quiet Cuban woman named Antonia, removed the bowls that had contained the gazpacho, a spicy chilled soup. Her presence brought a slight pause in the conversation.

"Where do your parents live, Barbara?" Lillian asked, sitting at the end of the table as hostess while Jock sat at the head.

"They are no longer living. They were killed in an air crash five years ago," she explained quietly.

"Five years ago," Todd repeated sitting opposite her. "I didn't realize that. You were still flying as a stewardess then."

"Yes."

"Is that when you asked to be transferred?"

"No. I continued flying for almost a year, until I got the shakes," Barbara admitted. "I came to believe that what goes up must come down."

"You became afraid of flying," Jock concluded.

"In a way. But I can quote you all the statistics that prove flying is much safer than driving on our highways." She smiled in self-mockery.

"But the skies are getting crowded," Lillian insisted.

"Not as crowded as the streets. When an airliner goes down with two hundred people aboard, that's news. And it's flashed all over the world. But two hundred cars can crash with two hundred people in one day and it isn't spectacular enough to be reported. Now if one car with two hundred people in it crashed, that would be a different story," she joked with irony.

"If you are convinced flying is safe, why are you afraid?" Jock questioned.

"Fear isn't always rational," she answered with a shrug. "Everyone who flies usually gets these attacks—pilots, stewardesses, navigators. Normally they have a lot of air miles logged, more than I did. It goes away. I just transferred before mine did."

"Your parents' accident was probably a contributing factor," Lillian surmised.

"Possibly. I know the schedule, the jetlag, the layovers in strange cities were all getting to me. After my parents died I began wanting a home again—not a room where I slept between flights. I wanted to have a place of my own, somewhere that I belonged." *And someone to belong to,* she could have added.

"You don't have any other family?" Lillian asked with a gently sympathetic look.

"No." Barbara shook her head, black curls moving with a silken gleam.

"You have mine," Todd inserted, and smiled ruefully, "Such as it is."

For the life of her, Barbara couldn't think of a suitable comment to Todd's statement. Luckily, his mother spoke up to prevent what would have been an awkward silence.

"You are a welcome addition to this family, Barbara. I liked you on sight," she told her and elaborated thoughtfully, "When I first saw you, I had the craziest feeling that I'd known you all my life."

Shock drained the color from Barbara's face. Those were the same words Jock had said when he walked up to her on the beach. Two seconds later he was kissing her. Her hand jerked in reaction to Lillian's phrase, knocking the water goblet over and spilling the contents on the white linen tablecloth. Ice water dripped on her lap, wakening Barbara to what she had done.

"Oh, my gosh!" she breathed in sharply, but Lillian had already righted the glass and Todd was mopping up the water with his linen napkin. "I'm sorry."

"It was only water," Lillian assured her. "Did I say something to upset you?"

"No. That is . . . ." Barbara slid a furtive look at Jock. Was he pale beneath his tan, or was it her imagination? "Someone else said that same thing to me once and . . . . I'm sorry I spilled the water."

"It will dry," the older woman insisted.

"Especially in this heat," Todd volunteered and shifted the topic of conversation to a discussion of the weather.

Somehow Barbara managed to get through dinner and the coffee in the living room afterward. Not until ten o'clock could she safely excuse herself without raising any eyebrows. It was a relatively chaste good-night kiss she gave Todd in the foyer before climbing the stairs to her room.

Bruised. She had been willing to accept that description of the condition of her heart during the drive here. After seeing Jock again, Barbara knew it wasn't accurate. He had walked all over her heart, stomped it into the ground. The pain was still there, and very real.

There had been other times, before she met Jock, when she had imagined herself in love. First there had been an infatuation with her high-school sweetheart, but it had never matured. Shortly after she became a stewardess she had been pursued relentlessly by a handsome married pilot. She had been flattered by his ardent attention, but it was amazing how quickly his interest lagged when she was transferred to ground operations. Her pride was bruised by that, but not her heart, because she had never let herself be serious about him. After that it had been a football player. She nearly fell for him until she found out he was romancing another girl at the same time he was supposedly dating only her.

Those were disappointments, bruises, but none of them constituted a heartbreak. Deep emotions had to be involved for that. And that is what Jock had aroused. Barbara was scared, because she knew he could do it again. She didn't want to be taken to those heights attained by that love. She wanted to be safe, with both feet on the ground. It was that old irrational fear of falling again.

Barbara changed quickly into her nightclothes and switched off the light, surrounding herself with darkness. The heavy-posted bed swallowed her up. Barbara wondered if she could sleep.

She was lying on her stomach, the bed covers partially kicked off, when a hand at the small of her back gently shook her awake. Mumbling an incoherent protest, Barbara resisted the attempt. She was having a wonderful dream and she didn't want it to end yet.

But the hand was insistent and a familiar, husky voice added to its efforts. "Come on, lazybones. You would sleep until noon if I let you."

Rolling onto her side, Barbara arched her back in a feline way to keep in contact with the caressing hand. Her lashes lifted sleepily. A tiny smile of contentment touched her lips as her dream came to life at the sight of the man sitting on the side of her bed.

"Mmm, Jock." She ran a hand up the sleeve of his shirt to his shoulder. "How come you are dressed all ready? I thought we were going snorkeling ... or was it skin diving today?"

Her fingers curled around the column of his neck to pull him down. Her sleep-drugged senses were unaware of the glint in his eyes. It was the strong, mobile mouth that claimed all her interest before it came down in moist possession of her lips. Pleasure erupted within her in a gold shower of bliss-filled sensations. Jock lifted her until her head and shoulders were resting on the plump pillow.

Both of her arms now circled him to let her hands glide familiarly over his strong, well-muscled back. A wild fire seared through her veins with a glorious heat. It spread through her nerve ends, making them come alive to his nearness. When he dragged his mouth from hers and lifted his head, her hands came to the front of his chest.

Her eyes were slow to open as she sighed his name with longing. "Jock—"

"That was six months ago, honey," his voice mocked her. "This morning you are scheduled to tour the citrus groves with your fiancé, Todd. Remember him?"

The beautiful dream popped like the fragile bubble it had been. Hands that had been thrilling to the solid rhythm of his heartbeat now stiffened to keep him at bay. A stifled gasp of dismay became choked in her throat as Barbara saw the way she had humiliated herself.

"What are you doing here?" she cried brokenly. "Where's Todd?"

"Waiting for you at the sorting and grading sheds." With amusement Jock watched the abrupt change in her attitude, from blazing passion to fiery indignation in one lightning move. "I knew you would take advantage of the chance to sleep late, so I promised to take you to him before noon."

"Get out of this bedroom!" she cried in hoarse anger, and tried to appeal to his discretion. "What if your mother walks in here?"

"There's no worry. She isn't here." The slashing lines on either side of his mouth deepened in an arrogant smile. His gaze lowered to make a leisurely survey of the upper half of her body. "I didn't realize long-legged pajamas could be so provocative."

The top half of her pajamas consisted of pink lace, suspended by spaghetti straps and secured by silk ribbons tied in two bows between her breasts. The long bottoms were pink silk with a wide band of see-through pink lace down the outside seam. But Jock's interest was directed at the pink ribbons tied in small bows. A trailing end of one ribbon was trapped between his fingertips, his knuckles brushing the flimsy lace covering a swelling breast.

"You always did enjoy making love in the mornings, didn't you?" he mused and untied the bow with hardly any effort.

"Don't." The one-word protest was all her breathless lungs would permit.

"That isn't what you said a minute ago." The second bow was undone with matching ease.

"Stop it, Jock." Her resistance was weakening despite the empty warning.

"Or what will you do, my dark-haired beauty?" With her breasts no longer confined by the lacy fragment of her top, his hand slipped beneath the material to mold his rough palm to the firm roundness of the underside of her breast, a thumb rubbing the sensitized peak. His lowering weight forced her elbows to bend as his warm breath teased her lips. "Will you whisper for help?" There was silent laughter in his murmured taunt.

Barbara turned her face into the pillow, fighting the melting weakness that wanted her to relax under his caress. The absence of her lips to possess didn't bother him. He nuzzled the sensitive hollow below her ear and nibbled at the delicate cord in her neck. Excited tingles danced over her skin in direct response. Barbara felt desire stirring and knew she had to stop him before she was overwhelmed by this inner upheaval.

She used his own words to do it. "I am engaged to your brother. Remember him?" It was a choked taunt, but its sting was just as sharp.

His caressing hands became punishing, abandoning her delectable curves to accidentally tangle his fingers in the lace material as they dug painfully into the soft flesh of her arms. She was half lifted off the pillow by the strength of his brutal grip. The savage gleam in his eyes warned Barbara that she had roused a sleeping tiger.

"You were mine before you ever became his!" With an abrupt release of his hold, Jock let her fall onto the pillow. His gaze raked her breasts with insolent possession while Barbara frantically sought to cover herself with the thin lace top, but he was already pushing himself from the bed to stalk to the door.

Stung by the callous way he had discarded her again, her pride demanded retaliation. "Get out of my room and stay out of it!" Barbara ordered in hoarse fury.

"No!" Jock whirled, his temper erupting like a golden storm. "This is my room! You are *my* guest! I own this house and all the land around it!" he thundered.

"Lillian—" Barbara attempted a defensive argument.

"My mother is here because *I* permit it! Let's get this clear." The volume of his voice was reduced to an ominous growl. "You are in *my* house and in *my* room. *I* say who stays or goes. No one else! So don't ever give me orders as to what I will do in my own home." A muscle worked convulsively in his jaw as he gathered his anger in check. "Be downstairs in fifteen minutes. We'll be riding to the sheds, so dress accordingly."

On that clipped order, Jock pivoted to stride to the

door. Her anger had been reduced to a tight ball of impotency. In desperation, Barbara grabbed the spare pillow and threw it at the closing door. It bounced harmlessly off the hardwood onto the floor. Her eyes burned with tears.

"I won't cry," she insisted fiercely. "I won't shed one more tear for you, Jock Malloy."

It took a lot of cold water from the bathroom faucet to cool the scorching liquid stinging her eyes. As much as Barbara would have liked to ignore it, there had been an implied threat in his command to be downstairs in fifteen minutes. If she wasn't, Jock was just as apt to come up and bring her down himself. That, and the knowledge that he was taking her to meet Todd, who was at present her only line of defense, made Barbara dress quickly in blue jeans, a T-shirt and boots. She was out of breath from hurrying by the time she reached the bottom of the stairs.

Pausing, she realized Jock hadn't said where he would be. She took a chance and tried the veranda. He was standing in the shadows, a shoulder leaned against an arch, a hand running tiredly over his jaw and throat. That impression of tiredness vanished in total alertness when he saw her. Barbara walked toward him, tilting her chin in vague challenge.

"I'm ready," she asserted.

"There's orange juice, coffee and some sweetbread on the table." He was curt with her as he motioned to the glass-topped table of wrought iron behind him.

"No breakfast?" She said it just to be difficult. Her normal appetite was stolen.

"You slept late," Jock reminded her. "You have a choice of having breakfast and spoiling the lunch Ramon's wife will be fixing for you and Todd, or—"

"Who is Ramon?" Barbara interrupted as she walked to the table to pour fresh-squeezed orange juice from the pitcher into a glass.

"One of my foremen. He's in charge of the fruit shipments. His house was practically a second home to Todd and me when we were younger." He was making an effort to sound civil.

It only irritated Barbara. "This Ramon works for you? He isn't family?"

"Everyone 'works' for me. Before that, they worked for my father. Before that, his father," he snapped. "That makes everyone on Sandoval land family—by loyalty if not by blood."

"You have a little feudal empire here, don't you?" she goaded. "With you the lord and master."

After throwing her a glowering look, Jock turned away. Barbara sensed if he hadn't, he might have been tempted to use physical violence. She shivered in reaction.

"That was uncalled for," she admitted. "I'm sorry, Jock. I don't know why I said it. I . . . suppose I wanted to make you angry . . . to pay you back."

"Forget it." He coldly dismissed her apology, stinging her pride once again. She stared at her glass of juice, wanting to throw it in his face. "What's it to be? Breakfast or lunch?"

"Lunch." She forced herself to swallow the orange juice, then set the empty glass on the table.

Her blue glance still held a shimmer of resentment at the way he had slapped away her apology. "I'm ready."

"No coffee or roll?" An eyebrow arched sharply to match the metallic edge of his look.

"No." She'd choke on it. "You said we would be riding."

"Mike is bringing the horses now." His announcement sent her glance to the treed lawn beyond the pool. A man was approaching the house leading two saddled horses, a blaze-faced chestnut and a gray. "Do you have a hat? The noonday sun can be fierce."

"No, I don't," While she was looking at the horses Jock had moved with that animal quietness she had forgotten he possessed. He had already put on his hat and was pulling it low on his forehead.

"I didn't think you would. Here's one of my mother's." The hat in his hand was cream-colored with a flat crown and brim. "See if it fits." He handed it to her and waited.

Under his watchful eyes, Barbara set it on her head. It fit snugly over her black curls and forced them to frame her face in their soft feathers. She pushed away the ones that tickled her temple and forehead, tucking them under the hatband. Finished, she turned for his inspection.

"How is that?" Her head was thrown back in challenge.

His gaze didn't stop with the hat. It continued downward to assessingly roam over the jutting curve of her breasts against the thin knit fabric of her

T-shirt. Barbara sucked in her breath in disturbed reaction to the stripping touch of his eyes on her stomach and waist, over her hips and down narrow-legged jeans.

"I brought the horses, Jock," a man called, snapping the invisible thread that had bound Jock's gaze to her.

Without a word to her, Jock turned and walked to the end of the veranda where the grass grew to the edge of the tile. The big, muscled gray horse whickered at the sight of him, pricking its ears in his direction. Barbara was slow to follow Jock, not recovering as quickly as he had. The man holding the reins of the two horses was about her age and height, with a fresh, open face and candid blue eyes that didn't attempt to hide the admiration in his look when he saw her up close. Although Barbara couldn't see Jock's face, he had obviously noticed the man's interested look.

"This is Mike Turbot. Barbara Haynes." Jock threw out the introductions with hard indifference. "Give her Sebring," he commanded and took the reins of the gray. "While she's here the chestnut will be at her disposal, but I don't want her riding alone."

"Yes, sir." The puzzled look the wrangler flashed Jock indicated he wasn't used to such curtness coming from him. "Here you are, Miss Haynes." Mike Turbot passed Barbara the reins and held the chustnut's bridle while cupping a hand under her elbow to help her into the saddle. Jock was already aboard the big gray, stepping into the stirrup and swinging into the saddle all in one fluid motion.

"Thank you, Mike." Because of Jock's rudeness, her smile was a little warmer than it might have been, as a feeling of compassion surfaced.

"Anytime, miss." He smiled and touched the curved point of his hat brim.

Jock had already reined the gray gelding away from the veranda to walk it across the thick carpet of lawn. Barbara's chestnut mount was more lightly built. It whirled gracefully at a touch of the rein on its sleek neck and glided after the horse and rider in a smooth, effortless walk. Spirited but well-trained, the horse was a joy to ride, but the tight-lipped profile of the man riding beside her kept Barbara from expressing her enthusiasm.

The pace was kept to a walk as they crossed the lawn rather than have the metal shoes of the horses dig out clumps of lush grass. Twice Barbara had to dodge a draping curtain of Spanish moss that bearded the massive oak trees shading the lawn. A white paddock gate stood open and the gray horse went through it at a trot. With a touch of the heel, Barbara's chestnut picked up the pace, too.

When Todd had mentioned riding to her, she had looked forward to the opportunity with pleasure, but Jock's grim silence was turning it into an ordeal. She was too conscious of his rough-hewn features set in such unyielding lines to enjoy the feel of the horse beneath her. It was like being given a banana split on a full stomach and being ordered to eat it all.

A barbed-wire fence blocked their way. Without dismounting, Jock maneuvered the gray horse close to a gate Barbara hadn't noticed and unhooked it, fastening it again after they had both gone through the opening.

As they started out again, Barbara couldn't stand the silence any longer. "I didn't know you were Todd's brother. Believe me, if I had, I would never have come here." Her voice trembled with the vibrant force of her conflicting emotions. "You gave me the impression you owned a ranch and I—"

"I do," Jock interrupted smoothly, not bothering to look at her.

"Your definition of a ranch and mine don't coincide. I wasn't thinking of orange groves and racehorses." There was a faintly sarcastic bite to her response. "A ranch to me means cattle—"

"That isn't a water buffalo." With a nod of his head, he directed her attention to his right.

A big Brahman bull stood in the shade of a tree, his massive humpbacked shape concealed until that moment by the mottled brown of his coat and the shadows of the thick limbs overhead. The bull twitched a drooping ear at a buzzing insect, his curved horns turning as his small dark eyes watched them ride by.

"Okay, so you run a few cattle." Barbara shrugged her shoulders in a vague dismissal.

"Over fifty thousand head, counting stock cattle and feeder steers," Jock informed her with a cool glance. "More than likely there are a couple thousand head running wild in the swamp that should be carrying the Sandoval brand."

Her mouth dropped open mentally, if not physically. With new awareness, her eyes encompassed the wild pasture they were riding through. It seemed to go on forever.

"How big is this place?" she murmured.

"It covers around two hundred and twenty thousand acres, a thousand of it in citrus trees and five hundred for the thoroughbreds. The rest is all cattle. I have about seventy-five people working for me. This operation is small compared to the Deseret Ranch or the Lykes Brothers. Surprised?" he mocked.

Barbara couldn't deny it. "I didn't know there were ranches this large in Florida."

"There have been ranches in Florida, and cowboys, before the first white man ever discovered there were tumbleweeds in Texas. Ponce de Leon brought the first boatload of Andalusian cattle here in 1521. The shoot-outs, the lynchings, the rowdy saloons were all romanticized in Westerns, but it all happened here first." His gaze skimmed her face with wicked arrogance. "Driving cattle across palmetto prairies, fighting wolves and malaria fever and swamp mire that would suck up a full-grown steer, sitting around a camp fire beneath trees ghostly draped with moss didn't appeal to the Zane Greys and Remingtons who built the myth of the cowboy."

"Florida is oranges, Disney World and Miami Beach, not cowboys." Barbara's image of her native state was undergoing a whole new evaluation.

"Cow hunters or cracker cowboys, that's what they were usually called. Cow hunters for the obvious reason that so much of this land was unfenced that they had to hunt the high grasses, swamps and cypress forests for the cows. Cracker cowboy comes from the rawhide whips they carried—'' Jock's hand touched the side of his saddle and Barbara noticed the coiled whip tied there ''—and the cracking sound the whip made that could be heard for miles when the cowboys were rounding up cattle. The three things a cowboy needed then he still needs today—a good horse, a whip and a good cow dog.''

''And Sandoval Ranch is yours.'' Barbara looked at him. She had always been aware of the strength in him, but now she saw the command the heavy responsibility of being in charge of all this resting easily on his broad shoulders.

''Yes.'' In that single word there was a wealth of pride and possession, understated and simple.

Barbara remembered his earlier reference to his inheritance of the land. ''It's been in your family for generations.''

''In the Malloy family, yes. My father left it to me when he died, just as Todd's father left him the hotel on that expensive strip of sand.''

The reference to Todd brought silence. The ground beneath their horses became marshy and Jock angled the gray gelding toward a raised strip of land. It was a dike to hold back the seeping waters of a cypress pond. As Barbara rode the chestnut along the crest, her gaze wandered over the raw, wild beauty of the exposed and tangled roots of the cypress giants. Primitive and unspoiled, it was no different from what it had been a hundred—two hundred years ago.

Where the pasture ground became firm again, Jock reined his mount down the sloping side of the dike. Barbara followed, her saddle shifting slightly beneath her. It affected her balance for only an instant, but Jock noticed it and reined his horse to a stop.

"I'll tighten the cinch," he stated, swinging out of his saddle and forcing Barbara to do the same.

She stepped to one side as he flipped her stirrup across the saddle seat to tighten the girth.

CHAPTER FOUR

HIS HEAD WAS BENT to the task, his masculine profile sculpted out of teakwood, hard grained and strong. Barbara watched him, her hand absently stroking the silken hip of the chestnut gelding, its feel reminding her of Jock's tautly muscled flesh. Sunlight glistened in the brown hair curling near the collar of his shirt. The impulse was strong to run her fingers through its sensuous thickness. She balled her hand into a fist to resist the almost blatant invitation.

"I take it you didn't tell Todd about me." The lightning shaft of his glance stabbed her in accusation.

Barbara stiffened defensively. "He knows there was another man, but I never told him who."

"Why?" Jock let the stirrup fall and turned to face her, resting an arm on the cantle.

"Why should I?" she flashed. "I may be engaged to him, but that doesn't give him the right to know the name, date and place of every man I've ever gone out with. Todd knows I've ... been with another man, but he doesn't expect a graphic description of who, what and where. And I don't expect him to tell me about the women he's been with."

"The circumstances have changed. Or hadn't you

noticed?'' His low voice was dry with challenge.

"How could I know you would turn out to be Todd's brother?'' Barbara replied sharply, all her raw tension surfacing. ''He kept referring to you as J.R. and he never said anything about different fathers and last names. The way he talked about this place, I thought it was a citrus farm. And you, you never said anything about having a brother. I can't remember you mentioning anything about your family. You were always too busy—'' The rest of the sentence became lodged in her throat.

But Jock finished it. ''—making love to you.''

"Yes,'' she snapped, unnerved by the way he was studying her with half-closed eyes.

"Are you sleeping with Todd?'' It was a shot from the hip that drew blood.

"No!'' And Barbara immediately wished she had told Jock it was none of his business. Instead she had to defend her answer. ''I'm not so rash anymore. I don't race blindly into a relationship or a man's bed since I met you.''

"Good.'' Jock straightened away from her saddle and Barbara took it as an indication he expected her to mount.

She wanted back in the saddle with the solidness of the chestnut beneath her instead of legs that were trembling. But when she took the step forward to mount, his arm crossed in front of her to block the movement. Barbara found herself enclosed in a trap. She leaned away from any contact with his hard, lean frame and closer to the saddled horse.

"Good, because I would hate to be put in a position where I would have to beat up my own brother for taking what was mine.''

"I'm not yours." Her denial was taunt and breathless, the wary blue of her eyes darting over the complacent expression on his rugged face, a face that was much too close.

"Regardless of that ring on your finger, you gave me rights over you six months ago." His hand touched her shoulder, then glided to her throat to stroke the underside of her chin with his thumb. Her pulse surged and fluttered madly at the caress. She was taking deep breaths to control the excited tightening of her stomach.

"Stop pretending that I was anything more to you than a one-night stand!" she protested stridently, needing to remind herself as much as him of the fact.

"One night?" Jock taunted with a roguish glint in his look.

She choked. "What does it matter how many? It was just a fling, a way to pass the time."

"A highly pleasurable way, wasn't it?"

"No." Which was an outright lie that challenged him.

When Barbara realized his intentions, her hands came up to ward him off, but it was already too late. His mouth was on hers, his hand cupped to her neck and his thumb digging under the point of her chin to prevent her from eluding his searching kiss.

Her hands strained against his chest to keep his body at a distance, but it took more effort to ignore the pleasant sensation of male sinew and bone beneath her fingers. When the hard point of his tongue probed the tightly closed line of her lips, a response quivered through her. Barbara fought it and his seductive insistence.

"Open your mouth," he growled against her lips, filling her lungs with his breath. It was warm, drugging air that muddled her already hazy thinking. "Open it, honey."

"No." And the door was opened to admit the piercing sweetness of his erotic kiss.

It enflamed her, burning up her paper-thin control. His arms went around her to gather her close and Barbara melted into his embrace. She was riding a shooting star, arching high in the heavens, and she didn't care when it might come down. Jock's hands had slid beneath her T-shirt to explore her skin and start their own fires.

The blood running through her veins became molten lava, a primitive heat that gelled everything in its path. A hand slipped inside the waistband of her denims to the hollow of her spine and arched her to his thrusting hips. Her fingers became hungry for the hair-roughened texture of the skin beneath his shirt and forced their way inside to let springy chest hairs tickle her sensitive palms.

The fiery comet she was riding was climbing too high. The crash to earth and reality would be too devastating. Barbara had to get off. She dragged her lips from his and shuddered as his mouth scorched her jaw and throat.

"It's over between us, Jock," she insisted in a tormented whisper. "Why can't you let it die? Why can't you forget?"

"Can you forget?" he demanded hoarsely, a

rough gravelly edge to his low voice. "Can you forget what it's like to have my hands on you? To have my kisses wash your flesh? Can you?"

Barbara groaned in answer because she couldn't forget. That was her punishment. The raw, wild memories lived with her, as intimate as their affair had been. She had survived its ending, but could she endure this attempt to revive it? Her eyes were tightly closed, trying to shut him out. But Jock would have none of it. His hands shook her roughly.

"Look at me!" he commanded. "You want me the same way I want you. Look at me and deny that's the truth."

The violent shaking forced her to look at him. Her tortured gaze went from the gold glaze of his eyes to the well-cut mouth still warm from her lips down to the rumpled and unbuttoned front of his shirt. She had done that, fought aside his shirt to reach that naked male flesh. Barbara couldn't deny the truth. She had lost her pride and self-respect in her abandoned response to his embrace. So she clung to the one good thing that had happened to her.

"I love Todd," she whispered. Todd, whose gentleness had helped her off her knees and made her lift her chin. Todd, who made her feel safe and protected, not threatened by emotions she couldn't control.

His mouth thinned into a ruthless line. The brutal grip of his fingers was gradually relaxed until Barbara was standing alone and he was stepping away.

"It isn't going to work, Barbara." He left her to walk to his horse.

For an instant she couldn't fathom his statement.

Then its meaning struck her and she reached for the saddle horn to keep from reeling. Her blue eyes were stark with pain and flat with discovery.

"You are going to tell Todd, aren't you?" she said.

"I am not a nameless nonentity who went in and out of your life." Jock's back was to her as he looped the reins over the gray's neck before mounting. "If you don't tell Todd about our affair, I will. We may have had different fathers, but he is my brother. Nothing has ever come between us before ... not until now. If you marry him, I'll never be able to look at you without remembering what went on between us before your marriage. Todd deserves to know why I'll be avoiding him in the future."

The tiny hope that Jock might keep their previous relationship a secret died a cold death. In her heart Barbara knew Todd had to be told. It was only fair. Now Jock had issued an ultimatum. If she didn't tell him, he would.

She climbed into the saddle and gave the chestnut its head. It followed the gray gelding when Jock started it forward. Her shoulders sagged under the weight of her decision. She didn't notice the pastures of high grass give way to orderly rows of fruit trees. When her horse stopped in front of a metal building, Barbara heard the murmur of voices and the hum of machinery.

"Where's Todd?" It was Jock who asked the question, and Barbara turned in her saddle to see him talking to an elderly man.

"Here he comes." The man gestured to the yawning door of the building.

Todd was walking toward her, all smiles and gladness. "I was beginning to wonder what had happened to you."

He reached up to span her waist with his hands and lift her from the saddle. Barbara was too numbed to refuse his assistance. Her wide, troubled eyes searched his handsome face as he set her on the ground. When Todd bent his head to kiss her, the gray horse snorted, sharply reminding Barbara of Jock's presence. Before Todd's mouth brushed hers, she turned away.

"I'm sorry I'm late," she apologized stiffly. "I overslept."

"You needed the rest." But his brown eyes had narrowed to study the lines of stress in her face. Todd smoothly concealed the look when he lifted his gaze to Jock. "Thanks for bringing her over here, J.R."

"Don't thank me, Todd. You might regret it." Jock's answer was terse, its message a mystery to his brother but not to Barbara. "I'll see you later at the house." He jabbed a heel into the gray's belly and the horse bounded forward into a canter.

Barbara slid a glance at Todd's puzzled expression as he watched Jock ride away. She wished that he didn't have to know the truth, that things could be the way they were before they had arrived here at the ranch.

"Come on. I'll show you around the shed." He was smiling again when he looked at her.

Gathering the threads of her courage, Barbara shook her head to refuse the invitation. "Not now. There's something I have to tell you first."

"Can it wait?" Todd asked with a quizzical expression. ''Ramon is free now to guide you through the place, but he's tied up later. We're having lunch with Ramon and his family.''

''Yes, Jock mentioned that,'' she admitted and took a breath to continue her explanation.

''You'll like Ramon. He's like an uncle to J.R. and me. We slept as many nights at his place as we did at the ranch house when we were kids—''

''Todd,'' she broke in impatiently. ''Please, I have to talk to you.''

''You make it sound urgent.''

''It is. I . . . I'm sorry about Ramon, but this isn't going to be easy and I don't want to put it off.'' She might not find the courage to tell him if she had to wait.

''Okay.'' His caressing hand was absently rubbing her spine but it didn't have the power to provoke a searing response. His touch was pleasurably sane. ''Let me introduce you to Ramon, then we'll go walk in the grove.''

Ramon Morales was the elderly man Jock had questioned. His dark eyes were sharply intelligent and the smile he gave Barbara was warm. On another occasion she would have enjoyed meeting him, but now she was too tense to show more than polite courtesy to him.

''I'm sorry, but something has come up that Barbara needs to talk to me about,'' Todd explained. ''I'm sure she would have learned much more from you, but I'll take her through the operation later.''

''You will come to lunch?'' Ramon questioned.

''Of course,'' Todd insisted, but Barbara wondered if he would want to after he heard what she had to say.

After apologizing again for keeping Ramon from his work, Todd promised to meet him at his house. Barbara's stomach was churning as they walked away from the man toward the trees. The air was heavily scented with oranges, weighted down by the hot sun. A faint breeze stirred the green leaves of the stunted orange trees. Barbara would have continued walking, but once they were out of sight of the sheds, Todd stopped.

''Would you like to explain to me what it is that's upset you?'' he probed gently.

She moved a step beyond him before halting. Her nervous hand reached to trace the round circumference of an orange. ''The man I had an affair with—''

''That's in the past, Barbara,'' Todd interrupted. ''I thought we had agreed to forget about it.''

''You don't understand,'' she breathed in agitation. ''That man was Jock.''

It was out and she suddenly couldn't breathe. Unwillingly Barbara turned to see the look of stunned shock and disbelief on his face.

''There must be a mistake,'' he murmured.

''I wish there was,'' Barbara replied in a stark voice. ''I didn't know he was your brother. I never connected Jock Malloy with the brother you called J.R. I assumed you had the same last names. If I had known—'' What was the use? She hadn't known. Now it was too late. The diamond ring sparkled on her finger in a silent reminder. Barbara took hold of it and pulled it off. ''You'll want this back.''

"No." His hand covered hers, folding the ring into her palm while his brown eyes searched her face. "I don't want it back unless you want to give it back. Do you still love him, Barbara?"

"I—" She shook her head mutely, unable to answer that question. The conflict of her heart and mind must have been expressed in her eyes, because Todd wrapped her in his arms and held her tight, resting his chin on the top of her black curls. "He was going to tell you," she mumbled into his shirt. "I had to tell you before Jock did."

"How does he feel about you?"

"He still wants me." The admission came out in a bitter laugh.

"And you?"

"Oh, he can still make me want him." It was a self-deprecating answer, exposing her shame. It brought a sob to her throat, but she took a deep breath and forced it down. As much as she wanted the comfort of Todd's arms, she couldn't in good conscience accept it. She firmly pried herself away from his chest. "I can't stay here, Todd. I have to leave."

"No. You are wrong. You have to stay and you have to face him," he insisted. "Hiding won't do any good. After a bad fall, you have to get back on the horse."

"But not the same horse!" Barbara protested.

"What happened, Barbara? Between you and J.R., I mean. You said he didn't want you around anymore. I know my brother can be harsh at times, but not totally insensitive in the way you have made him sound." He frowned.

"In his way, I suppose he let me down easy. Jock

just didn't know how far I had to fall," she said, trying to laugh but not succeeding very well. It hadn't been funny. Even in retrospect, it wasn't now. "After he'd asked me to come with him to his ranch—Sandoval, as it turns out—I refused for all the reasons I've already told you. Later on that same day, I went into the bedroom and found him packing to leave...."

Barbara could remember it all so clearly, walking into the bedroom, seeing him folding his shirts so neatly and laying them in the suitcase. A sweet pure love had seared her. She had walked up behind him and wound her arms around his middle to hug his back. Jock had stopped packing to half turn. Barbara had ducked under his raised arm to be held in his embrace. Instead of kissing her as she had expected, he had locked his hands behind her back for a moment and looked down at her. If he had repeated his previous invitation, she would have accepted in a flash.

Jock hadn't. Instead, he had unwound her arms from around him and held her hands in front of him. For the rest of her life, she would hear the words of rejection he had uttered then. "I have enjoyed being your lover, Barbara, but it's time we became friends."

"Every nerve in her body had screamed with pain at the statement. Somehow she had managed to force out a husky laugh and pull her hands from his loose hold to turn away. Jock hadn't attempted to stop her. She had been dying with love for him and he had been casually asking to become her friend.

Barbara couldn't remember now exactly how she

had responded. Something to the effect that she couldn't be friends with someone like him, so why not just make it a clean goodbye. It was fun while it lasted, but it was over.

The rest was a blur of pain. Jock had mentioned calling her the next time he was in Miami, but Barbara wasn't going to become a name and phone number in his black book. So she said, "Don't call me, I'll call you." A trite phrase, but she had meant it.

All of that she explained to Todd in considerably less detail. "I never meant to come between you and Jock. Please believe that," Barbara concluded.

"I do," Todd assured her.

"Jock was right about one thing, though," Barbara sighed. "You can't marry me. How could you face him knowing that he and I—"

"No. Don't think about me," he interrupted, catching her chin and lifting her face for his examination. "Could you face him as my wife?"

"I thought I could. But now . . . I'm not sure."

"We have never been lovers, Barbara. Perhaps if we—"

But she suddenly jerked away from his hand. She knew what Todd was about to suggest and she couldn't. If he made love to her now, she knew she would compare him to Jock. She knew she would come away from it dissatisfied and wanting. Before she had thought it was the commitment she was afraid of, but now she realized she had avoided intimacy with Todd because she instinctively knew the enjoyment wouldn't be there. Without love, sex would be simply a physical act.

Didn't she love Todd? She needed him desperately. She needed his kindness, his gentleness, but did she love him? The emotion he aroused in her was insipid compared to the thundering glory Jock caused. Barbara doubled her hands into fists. She cared enough about Todd to learn to love him. Maybe never as wildly as she loved Jock, but she didn't want to be that crazy about anyone again. It hurt too much.

"It's too soon, Todd," Barbara protested brokenly.

He caught her by the arms and held her when she tried to turn away. "I have never asked you to do anything for me, but I'm asking now. I want you to stay here for these two weeks and get my brother out of your system once and for all."

"What if I don't, Todd?" She voiced the fear that was so strong within her.

"Then you can give my ring back," he said flatly. "It will be a trial period, a testing period if you will. In the meantime we'll carry on as usual. Which includes lunch with Ramon and his wife."

"Todd ...." Her dark head made an uncertain movement.

"Two weeks isn't a lifetime."

But it will seem like it, she thought. "No, of course, it isn't," she agreed for his benefit.

"Come on. We'll walk over to Ramon's house. It isn't far from here." He put an arm around her shoulders and started walking back the way they had come.

Ramon Morales and his wife, Connie, were a warm, friendly couple who welcomed Barbara into

their home as if she was already a member of the
family. She could well understand why Todd and
Jock regarded it as their second home. The couple
naturally regaled her as Todd's fiancée, with tales
from his childhood. It was inevitable that Jock's
name would be included in the stories.

After lunch, Barbara volunteered to help the older
woman wash the dishes while Todd and Ramon
walked out to the groves behind the simple wooden
structure. The warmth of the kitchen made Barbara
feel at home, less of an intruder.

"You are lucky, Barbara." Connie Morales
rinsed a plate under a faucet. "Todd will make a very
understanding husband."

"Yes, I think so, too," she agreed, ignoring the
twinge of guilt she experienced.

"Two brothers couldn't be more different than
Jock and Todd. As boys, the differences were much
more striking. Jock never learned to share his toys.
What was his was his," she declared with a raised
eyebrow for emphasis, "and woe to those who tried
to play with something that belonged to him. The
Malloy wrath fell on them with a vengeance. Todd
gave his toys away. He had the softest heart. Stray
animals found their way to his doorstep. If they were
hurt, Todd took them to Jock and—"

"To Jock?" Barbara interrupted with surprise.

"Oh, yes, he has healing hands. Todd found the
hurt animals, Jock cured them, and Todd loved
them. All except once," the woman remembered
with a pause. "Jock accidentally backed the car over
a puppy one time. He set its broken leg and took it
home with him. It's the only dog I've ever known

that was allowed to sleep in the house. It had a rug at the foot of Jock's bed. The two were almost inseparable until the dog finally died of old age.''

''When was that?'' she asked curiously.

''It must be almost four years ago now. When Blue died—that was the dog's name, a blue heeler—Jock wouldn't take another dog with him when he went out to check cattle. As far as I know, he still doesn't. I never really thought about it until this moment.'' Connie Morales paused in her dish washing to look at Barbara.

''Todd always had a menagerie of pets around him with love enough for all, but Jock had only the one.'' With an unconcerned shrug, she returned to her washing. ''As I said, they were as different as night and day. And still are.''

Totally different. Barbara couldn't agree with the woman more. It showed in other ways, too. Todd loved the hotel business, constantly meeting new faces, the atmosphere changing with each convention. The variety, the whirl, the social life were important elements in his life. And Jock ran this small empire, a caretaker of the land and its people. He followed the deep-seated tradition of the soil.

Barbara wasn't certain she wanted to learn this much about either man. In two weeks she might have to walk away from both of them. In two weeks she could carry a lifetimes of memories away with her. She wished she hadn't agreed to stay, but Todd had asked so little from her and had given so much.

After the dishes were washed, Todd came in and Barbara bade the couple goodbye and promised to see them again before she left. She received the tour through the sorting and shipping sheds. When Todd explained about the different grading of fruit, she appeared to listen, but her mind was miles away. If Todd noticed her lack of attention, he didn't comment on it.''

Her chestnut horse and a mahogany bay were tied outside the sheds when they completed the tour. The route Todd took her on back to the house was different from the way Jock had brought her. It was longer, more scenic, abundant with wildlife and colorful birds stalking marshland pools. With Todd, Barbara was able to relax. When she was with Jock, she was never sure when the world would erupt around her.

CHAPTER FIVE

As BARBARA DESCENDED the stairs to the first landing, she met Lillian Gaynor on the way up. She hadn't seen the woman all day. Lillian hadn't been in the house when she and Todd had finally returned. Barbara had gone directly to her room and taken a leisurely bath to soak away the horsey smell and dress for dinner.

"You look lovely, Barbara." Lillian paused on the stairway to admire the accordion-pleated caftan of wild silk.

"Thank you." It was a little dramatic, but it fit her mood.

"I understand from Jock that you've had a busy day—lunch with Ramon, a tour of the citrus operation and a horseback ride," she remarked with a broad smile.

"Yes, I have." Barbara didn't have to ask when Lillian had seen Jock. She'd heard him come upstairs an hour before and the rush of water running in a shower. And she had recognized the sound of his footsteps when he'd left his room to go downstairs. She expected that he was out on the veranda now.

"I hope you like Connie. She is a dear friend, and

like a second mother to my sons," Lillian explained.

"Both Connie and Ramon made me feel like one of the family already," Barbara admitted.

"They seem like family. John and Ramon were like brothers. John was Jock's father, John Randolph Malloy," Lillian explained. "Ramon provided me with a very strong shoulder to lean on when I lost John so suddenly. And Connie . . . well, she simply took over running the house and looking after Jock until I could handle it again."

"I can imagine."

"Goodness, what am I thinking about, keeping you talking on the stairs like this," Lillian admonished herself with a laugh. "Here comes Todd downstairs and I haven't even made it to my room yet. You will all have a head start on me if I don't hurry."

"Hello, mom. Are you coming or going?" Todd stopped on the step behind Barbara, casually resting a hand on her shoulder.

"Going," she laughed. "I'll see you two on the veranda in about twenty minutes. Save me a drink."

"We will," Todd promised. As his mother passed him to climb the last flight of stairs to the second floor, Barbara started to proceed down them. Todd's hand tightened on her shoulder to stop her. She glanced back at him in surprised question. His dark head bent to nuzzle her neck. "You smell delectable, darling."

Darling? He'd never used any term of endearment before, Barbara thought with a start. She could hardly object, being his finacée. So why did it make her uneasy?

"I found some perfumed bath salts," she said, to explain the musky scent that clung to her skin. "I got a little carried away."

"It's very provocative," Todd murmured. "But so are you."

His mouth teased her lips with a feather kiss, but they didn't tremble in response. Barbara felt almost guilty at that. Todd had always been affectionate, but never as loverlike as he was behaving at the moment. Was he putting his suggestion of the morning into deed?

The irony of it suddenly struck Barbara. One brother, who was her dearest friend, wanted to become her lover and husband. The other brother, who had been her passionate lover, had wanted to become her friend. There was some twisted humor in that somewhere. It was a pity she couldn't find it.

It was impossible for Todd not to sense her lack of participation in his attempted caress. Concealing a sigh, he lifted his head and flashed her a forgiving smile. Then he was releasing her shoulder so she could continue down the steps while he followed.

"Have I told you how beautiful you look?" His hand curved possessively on her waist then they reached the foyer.

"No, but my ego would love to hear it." She needed some bolstering, she thought, as she turned toward the veranda doors.

"You do look beautiful. And if I'm lying, may I

turn into a frog,'' Todd vowed and made a muted croaking sound in his throat.

Barbara laughed, as she was supposed to do, the tension flowing out of her for a few short minutes. Todd reached in front of her to open the veranda door and Barbara walked through, a smile remaining on her face as a result of the laughter he had induced. It started to fade when she came under the glittering scrutiny of a pair of tawny eyes. She had the feeling she had become the target of some predatory beast about to spring on her at any second. Todd's arm was around her waist again, protecting her from attack. When she looked up at him, the smile came back, born by the feeling of relief and safety.

''Isn't it a rule of the house, J.R., that the first one at the drink cart has to play bartender?'' Todd's gaze pointedly noted the fact that Jock was standing in front of the cart with a drink in his hand.

On the surface Jock appeared relaxed and at ease, enjoying an early-evening cocktail while a slowly setting sun left a crimson stain in the sky. His hair glistened from the dampness of his shower, its rich chestnut gold thickness faintly unruly in a sensual sort of way. Unlike Todd, Jock didn't bother with a sports jacket. The brown silk shirt was unbottoned at the throat with the sleeves rolled up to expose tanned forearms. Cream-colored trousers molded his masculine length, his feet slightly apart in a stance that suggested command and readiness. Beneath that indolent facade, Barbara sensed violent, coiled energy waiting to be released.

''Your drinks are fixed. Scotch and water. Rum

and Coke.'' Ice clinked against the sides of the glass in his hand as Jock swung it toward the drink cart to indicate the filled glasses on the tray.

"Now that is service,'' Todd declared.

"I heard Barbara laugh and knew you were coming,'' Jock explained his foreknowledge with a dryly sweeping look at her.

"Thank you. It was a thoughtful gesture.'' A response seemed to be expected from her so Barbara gave a courteous one.

The languid, balmy air suddenly felt very warm and heavy, crushing at her lungs to make their efforts labored even if it didn't show. The closeness of the atmosphere reminded Barbara of the way it felt before an approaching storm front moved in, oppressive, sticky and much too still.

Jock didn't move out of the way as she walked with Todd to the decorative wrought-iron cart. The intimidation of his presence was strong. She wished for some armor to shield her from his piercing eyes, their force not affected by the thick veil of masculine lashes. Picking up her drink, Barbara turned and came in full contact with his gaze.

Her head came back in protective defiance. "Stop looking at me that way, Jock. Todd knows. I told him,'' she said stiffly.

His sharp gaze made a quick scan of her features, then swept down to the diamond glittering on her left hand before it shot swiftly to Todd. Cool and alert, Jock took a sip from the drink in his hand.

"How did you take the news, little brother?'' he taunted him over the rim of the glass.

"It didn't change anything." Todd shrugged smoothly. "Whatever there was between you and Barbara was six months ago. It's in the past and had nothing to do with today."

His lip curled derisively. "You must have told him one hell of a story, honey," he jeered.

"I told him the truth," Barbara retorted, stung by his insinuation.

"I know all about it," Todd confirmed her statement. "When you met and the time you spent together. You gave her a pretty raw deal, but it's over."

Jock tipped his head at an angle to study her through half-closed eyes. "I gave you a raw deal, did I?" Within that drawling comment there was something hot and biting. "Is that what you told him?"

"I'm sure it is a matter of definition and point of view." Her fingers tightened around the glass, its chill matching the one inside her. She stared into the dark surface of the liquid rather than continue to hold Jock's gaze. She knew the exact second his eyes left her. That tingling sensation of danger went away.

"She belongs to me, Todd. I want her back," Jock stated.

Just like that. As if she were some object a pair of children were squabbling over. Her head came up with a start, indignant fires glittering in her blue eyes. But neither man took any notice of her.

"You couldn't keep her so you lost her," Todd said. "Now it's a case of finders keepers. Your prior claim doesn't mean anything anymore. I found her. And I'm not going to let her go."

"This isn't a game!" Barbara protested angrily. "You aren't going to play tug-of-war with me. Neither of you!"

"Stay out of this!" Jock ordered sharply.

"No!"

"Barbara is right," Todd sided with her. "You can't have her back because she isn't mine to give. It's her choice to make."

"In that case, you might as well give his ring back to him now and save some time," Jock instructed with a flicking glance at Barbara.

"How typically arrogant of you!" she breathed in anger. "What makes you think I would prefer you?"

Jock made the half turn to confront her squarely and bring himself within a foot of her. That powerful magnetic aura that surrounded him sucked Barbara into its force field, trapping her as securely as if he'd taken her into his arms. The warm, clean smell of him suffocated her lungs while his dangerous virility sent the adrenaline surging through her veins, heightening all her senses.

"You don't really want me to answer that question in front of Todd, do you, honey?" His low voice was a husky taunting caress. "You don't want me to remind you of that first time we made love. Afterward you had bright, beautiful tears in your eyes because it had been so wonderful. Do you want him to hear how we made love outside with only the stars of a soft, southern night for company?"

"That's enough." It was a gasping plea for him to stop seducing her with memories. The wild yearning to be possessed by him again was throbbing through her veins and she couldn't let it take control.

A tigerish gleam of satisfaction glowed in his eyes. He had accomplished his objective—to make her cry out for mercy because he still had the power to make her want him without even having to touch her. All Jock had to do was make love to her in his mind, promise her with his eyes and tease her with his voice and she was trembling with searing desire.

"You have your answer, J.R.," Todd said calmly, putting an arm around Barbara and pulling her out of the invisible circle of Jock's attraction. "She doesn't want you so don't humiliate her anymore with memories of an affair she wants to forget."

"I'm not convinced that's what she wants. And neither is she," Jock replied lazily.

Barbara shivered, but Todd's arm absorbed the action. "I will want you to be best man at our wedding."

"You have to be out of your mind!" was the astonished and angry retort Jock issued.

"You'll have a year to get used to the idea," Todd countered and Barbara marveled at his calm. "You are my brother. I wouldn't want anyone else to be my best man."

"If you think I'm going to stand beside you while she walks down the aisle—" His mouth snapped shut on the sentence, his lips thinning in savage anger. Jock took a deep breath, his nostrils flaring.

"*If* she does marry you, you can be certain I'll have urgent business elsewhere on your wedding day, no matter what date you set. I'll never be able to accept her as a sister-in-law, Todd. Understand that now."

There was no reply forthcoming from Todd as Jock's warning hung heavy in the air. The spiked fronds of a leaf on the palm tree by the pool made a rustling sound, stirred by the first breath of the evening breeze. The door to the veranda opened and Lillian Gaynor walked through to join them.

The smile didn't leave her face as she walked toward them, but Barbara noticed the sudden alertness that leaped into her eyes. Her glance darted between the two men that were her sons.

"I have the feeling I'm entering a combat zone," she declared in a deliberately lighthearted tone. "Are you two arguing about something? Todd, fix me a planter's punch."

"Of course, mother." Todd's hand reassuringly squeezed Barbara's shoulder before he took his arm away to walk to the drink cart.

"Well?" Lillian said expectantly. "Is someone going to tell me what's going on or am I just going to be treated with silence?" She continued to smile, a maternal indulgence in the expression.

"When we were children, you always managed to settle our disputes. Maybe you can handle this one," Jock stated. "You see, I knew Barbara before Todd did. And I'm not willing to give up my prior claim to her."

It was obviously the last thing that Lillian

would have thought of that her sons would be quarreling about. Her startled gaze flew immediately to Barbara.

"You and Jock met each other before this weekend?" she asked for confirmation.

"Yes, but he doesn't have any prior claim to me," Barbara insisted. "We said goodbye several months ago."

"Several months ago?" Lillian echoed and turned to look at Jock with curious, questioning eyes.

"Here's your punch, mother." Todd handed her a tall glass, frosty on the outside. "Barbara didn't realize J.R. was my brother until she came here. That's why no one has mentioned any of this before. She told me today, afraid it might make a difference. But it doesn't to me."

"You are wrong, Todd," Jock inserted. "Because I'm going to take her back."

"Barbara isn't a toy, Jock," his mother admonished.

"Which is just as well because now you can't insist that I share her with Todd." His mouth twisted wryly into a smile.

"I think it's the other way around," Lillian corrected. "Barbara is engaged to Todd."

"Not for long," Jock replied with complacent certainty. "I'll win her back. I have the advantage over Todd in that I know all of her weaknesses. All I have to do is exploit them to the fullest." He lifted his glass in Barbara's direction, a toast of silent promise to carry out what he'd said. There was a mercurial rise in her pulse.

"You can try, Jock," Barbara returned in weak defense.

"I've arranged to have an engagement celebration after the riding competition Thursday night," Lillian stated, glancing at Jock. "If you and Todd are going to be at each other's throats, perhaps I should postpone it until the differences are finally settled between you two."

Diplomatically Lillian didn't indicate which one of her sons she thought would win or which she supported. She didn't even suggest that Todd's engagement to Barbara might be in jeopardy. The only concern she voiced was a desire to have the celebration be a happy one. Barbara admired her tact.

"Don't worry, mother. We aren't going to come to blows over this," Todd assured her.

"Don't be too sure about that, little brother." Jock took a sip of his drink and didn't glance at Todd before or after his remark. He kept his attention focused on the drink in his hand.

"I am certain," Todd replied. "This is Barbara's decision. She won't make it on the outcome of any fight between us."

"My practical, sensible brother," Jock declared cynically. "Sometimes I'm amazed that we are related."

"That's because you are so fiercely intense," his mother declared. "You can be very single-minded at times."

"That's why I always win," Jock pointed out. "Because I never let anything stand in my way. So go ahead with your plans for Thursday night to celebrate this temporary engagement of Todd and Barbara. We need an excuse for a party. It might just as well be that. Any objections?'' A raised eyebrow directed the question to Barbara.

''A hundred,'' she said in irritation. ''But go ahead with the party. No one listens to what I have to say anyway.''

''Maybe that's because you don't say what you are really feeling,'' Jock suggested with a glinting look.

''How do you know what I'm feeling?'' Barbara flared. ''You can't crawl inside my body!''

''I'd like to,'' he murmured.

''Jock.'' His mother's tone said he had gone too far.

Two quick blasts of a horn interrupted them. It was followed immediately by a slamming door and the sound of someone hurrying across the courtyard to the veranda arches. Everyone turned as the young wrangler, Mike Turbot, came into view.

''Jock, we've got a mare down. We called the vet a half an hour ago and he should be arriving any minute. She had a stillborn foal and she's starting to hemorrhage. Sunny said for me to get you right away.'' While Mike was rushing out his urgent message, Jock was already setting his glass down and letting his long strides take him across the veranda toward Mike and the courtyard.

''Don't wait dinner for me,'' Jock tossed over his shoulder as he followed the wrangler to the pickup truck waiting in front of the house, its engine still running.

WHEN JOCK DIDN'T RETURN to the house for dinner, Lillian had Antonia, the cook, fix some sandwiches and hot coffee and sent her to the foaling barn with them. "Jock will forget to eat otherwise," Lillian explained.

A little after ten o'clock, Todd suggested that they take a stroll in the moonlight and Barbara agreed. It was peaceful outside, the air holding a languid warmth. The moss-draped trees cast ghostly shadows in the light of a full moon. The Milky Way was a white gossamer ribbon of stars trailing across a midnight-blue sky. All was quiet as Barbara wandered beneath the oaks of the back lawn, her hand in Todd's. But her gaze kept straying to the buildings of the horse stables, white shapes in the night. Jock hadn't come back yet, and she couldn't help wondering how much longer he'd be. The realization drew a sigh. Even when he was out of her sight, he wasn't out of her mind.

"Tired?" Todd questioned the reason for her sigh.

"Yes, a little," she replied because she didn't want to admit the real cause for it.

"Would you want to go inside or stay up for a while?"

"I think I'd rather go inside to bed, if you don't mind." Barbara didn't want Todd to suspect or even think that she wanted to wait up for Jock. It was far better to pretend tiredness.

"I don't mind," Todd insisted and turned toward the creamy arches of the veranda. "It's been a tiring day—in one form or another.'' His lips brushed the springing waves of her black hair. ''Do you feel more relaxed after our walk?''

''Yes, very much so,'' she agreed.

As they neared the veranda, Barbara saw a small red light glowing in the shadow of an arch. It puzzled her until she caught the aromatic scent of burning tobacco and realized it was the red tip of a cigarette. Jock was on the veranda and her heart skipped a beat.

She stole a glance at Todd to see if he had noticed it, but he gave no sign. With the aid of the faint glow from the cigarette, she was just barely able to make out Jock's outline in the shadowy darkness of the arch. He was leaning a shoulder against the inside wall of the arch, gazing out into the night, although Barbara couldn't be sure if he was looking at them.

It was through another archway that they stepped onto the tiled veranda floor. Jock straightened, and the movement attracted Todd's gaze. He hesitated, then stopped, his hand closing tighter around Barbara's.

''How did it go with the mare, J.R.?'' Todd inquired.

An interior light in the house spilled through the windows to dimly illuminate the veranda. It was just enough to permit Barbara to see the smeared stains on Jock's light-colored trousers and notice wisps of straw clinging to his clothes. He had a glass in his hand, a short, fat one. Jock didn't immediately respond to Todd's question. With a flick of a forefinger he tossed the cigarette into the night's darkness, and swirled the dark liquid in the glass before downing it in one impatient swallow.

"The mare died twenty minutes ago," he announced flatly.

"That's too bad," Todd offered in sympathy.

"I'm sorry, Jock," Barbara inserted softly.

It was to her that Jock responded. "Are you?" Even in the semidarkness the slanted smile of mockery was visible.

"Yes." Her answer came back quick, drawn by his taunting skepticism.

He faced her, an invisible force seeming to reach across the distance for her. "Then come comfort me," his voice invited her into his arms.

For a charged second Barbara nearly succumbed to the temptation of his seductive request. All her nerves were poised for the command to accept and glide across the space to him. A strangled sound came from her throat.

Pivoting sharply to the house entrance, she pulled her hand free of Todd's and left a choked good-night behind to conceal her desperate flight. She raced into the house and up the stairs to her room. She heard Todd following and went into the private bathroom and turned on the sink faucet so she wouldn't hear his knock on her door. Coward, she called herself, but she didn't have the courage to face Todd. Even after he'd gone to his own room, Barbara let the water run to cover the sound of the dry sobs wracking her chest. But no tears fell.

A KNOCK AT HER BEDROOM DOOR was followed by Todd's voice asking, "Are you ready yet?"

"Almost!" Barbara shouted back her answer so it could be heard through the closed door and wiped at the streak of cinnamon lipstick that had strayed outside the curve of her lip. "Will I need a hat for church?"

"No. I'll meet you downstairs," he called.

"I'll be there in just a couple of minutes," she promised and heard his footsteps on the hardwood floor as he moved away from her door toward the staircase.

After running a brush through her black hair, she fluffed the thick, long curls with her fingers and stepped back to inspect her reflection. The summer linen suit of emerald green made a startling contrast to the black of her hair and pointed out the vivid blue of her eyes. Yet its trim lines carried a subdued elegance that seemed quite proper for attending the local church while still flattering her slim figure.

Satisfied with her appearance, Barbara turned away from the mirror and walked into her bedroom for the beige purse that matched her heeled sandals. Since Todd was already downstairs and waiting, she didn't linger and hurried into the hallway that surrounded the open stairwell. She had reached the first landing when she heard Lillian's voice in the foyer below.

"Aren't you coming to church with us, Jock?" she asked, and Barbara paused, not wanting to encounter Jock yet.

"I can't."

"It's Sunday. Do you have to work on the Sabbath?" his mother protested.

"Somebody forgot to tell Mother Nature this is a day of rest," Jock teased. "Another mare is foaling. I'm on my way to the barn as soon as I change clothes."

Barbara realized waiting had been useless. She wasn't going to be able to avoid Jock since he was on his way upstairs. She started down the steps and met him halfway.

"Good morning." His gold-flecked eyes quickly skimmed over her in a familiar fashion.

"Good morning," she murmured, trying to keep her gaze downcast without succeeding.

Jock deliberately blocked her path, forcing her to stop. Her pulse started beating rapidly in her throat. He noticed it and a smile twitched at his mouth.

"Say a prayer for me, will you, honey?" His fingertips touched her cheek, his thumb brushing her lips in a fleeting caress that was there, then gone, as he unexpectedly moved out of her way and continued up the stairs.

Having braced herself for some kind of an assault, it took her a second to realize he had left. Yet brief as the meeting had been, it had been equally disturbing. Barbara continued down the stairs, encased in a warm feeling she couldn't shake.

The small community church was an unpretentious steepled building of wood with stained-glass windows only in the area of the altar. The pews were old, made of hand-hewn polished cypress wood. The floor, too, was of hard cypress wood, except for a worn, carpeted runner down the center aisle. The church was hushed inside, a place of worship. No one used it for gossiping conversation, although Barbara noticed that Lillian Gaynor received many nods and smiles. She was obviously a familiar member of the congregation and well liked. The service was a simple one, the sermon short and filled with a message of God's love.

After the doxology, the minister stood at the door. The exodus from the church was slow. Todd spied a childhood friend and excused himself to go say hello. Barbara lingered with Lillian at the back of the line.

"This is a simple church, not nearly as grand as the ones in Miami," Lillian admitted, "but I prefer it."

"So do I," Barbara agreed.

"Jock's father and I were married here three weeks to the day after we'd met. It would have been sooner, but the minister was ill. J.R.—my husband — was furious about that." Lillian smiled and Barbara could tell by her expression that she was recalling happy memories. "His name was John Randolph Malloy, but everyone called him J.R. That's where Todd gets his nickname for Jock. When he was a toddler he heard people referring to Jock as J.R.'s son and just picked it up," she explained. "But my husband was quite a man. Once we'd met, he hardly gave me a chance to catch my breath. I never had time to say no, yes or maybe. Not that I wanted to, mind you," she laughed softly.

And Barbara understood the feeling. That's the

way it had happened to her with Jock. He had taken her up on cloud nine, three east of the Milky Way, and she hadn't wanted to come down ever. But he had finally pushed her off.

"I suppose you and Todd will be married in Miami," Lillian remarked.

"Yes, that's what Todd has discussed," she admitted somewhat absently. "All our friends are there," she added.

"Sebastian and I were married in Miami, too. Todd's father," she added in explanation. "It was a fancy affair with an enormous reception afterward. Sebastian thought I had missed out on that excitement of a big wedding." Her gaze strayed to the altar and Barbara had the impression the simplicity of Lillian's first wedding to Jock's father was a more precious memory. As if concerned that she had sounded partial, Lillian added, "Todd's father made me very happy. He was very good to me."

"Knowing Todd, I'm sure he was," Barbara murmured, understanding clearly that Lillian had not been swept off her feet by him as she had by her first husband. Barbara couldn't help drawing parallel comparisons between her reactions to Todd and Jock, and Lillian's to her two husbands, their fathers.

Todd rejoined them and the subject was diverted. "I mentioned to Frank about the engagement party on Thursday. He said he would come."

"That's wonderful," Lillian smiled.

"What is this riding competition you were talking about?" Barbara asked.

"It's a weekly get-together for the ranch hands. They compete between themselves in some jackpot roping and riding," Lillian explained. "A limited version of a private rodeo, strictly for our own benefit and pleasure. The cowboys get to show off their skills and have some fun. I think you'll enjoy it."

"I'm sure I will," Barbara agreed.

CHAPTER SIX

WHEN THEY RETURNED to the house after church, Jock wasn't anywhere around. The three of them had Sunday dinner without him. That afternoon Todd and Barbara walked to the foaling barns. Jock wasn't there, but they saw the mare and her hours-old foal, all legs and head.

Sunday seemed to set a precedent. With a ranch the size of Sandoval there was always something happening, something needing to be done, and a major or minor crisis cropping up that demanded Jock's presence. Except in the evenings, Barbara saw very little of him.

It was Todd who took her riding and introduced her to some of the foremen and their families who lived on the property. He showed her around and kept her entertained. This two-week vacation seemed to be going just the way they had planned it before she arrived and found Jock in residence.

Sunday, Monday and Tuesday had passed without incident. Jock's threat to win her back was proving to be an idle one. Since that meeting on the stairs, Barbara hadn't spoken to him alone. And in the evenings he had made no attempt to maneuver her out of Todd's company.

She was ... disappointed, Barbara realized. She had wanted Jock to pursue her and attempt to win her back. Not that she was admitting that she wanted him to succeed. Irritated, Barbara struck out across the pool in a vigorous crawl. When her outstretched hand struck the concrete side, she stopped to catch her breath, holding onto the edge while she pushed the wet black curls out of her face.

"Who are you racing against?" Todd laughed.

Barbara looked up in surprise. He stood near the side, fully clothed. "I thought you were going to change into your swim trunks and join me. Or do you intend to come in like that?" she accused, half in jest.

"No such luck. Mother has this long list of things she absolutely has to have for the party tomorrow night and I have been deputized to fill it. Instead of swimming, would you want to go into town with me?" he invited.

Barbara hesitated. It was a hot, sticky day, which was why she opted to swim after lunch. The prospect of leaving the cool waters of the pool to ride into town and walk up and down store aisles did not appeal to her.

"I'd rather stay here," she admitted.

"I don't blame you." Bending down, Todd cupped the back of her head with his hand and pulled her halfway to meet his descending mouth. His kiss was hard and long—passionate if she had been so inclined to respond. Barbara simply couldn't fake that desire, so she settled for not resisting his. Todd didn't appear disappointed by the kiss when he straightened. "I won't be gone long."

"Hurry back."

He disappeared through the arches into the courtyard. A few minutes later she heard a car going down the private lane.

She splashed and lazed around in the pool for a while longer until she finally tired and climbed out. She wiped the excess moisture from her skin with a long, thick beach towel, then laid it over a lounge chair and stretched out on it to let the hot sun dry her bikini and evaporate the water on her skin. Donning a pair of sunglasses, Barbara picked up the novel she'd brought along and began reading.

The exercise and the hot sun made her drowsy, and the book wasn't really holding her interest. Giving up, Barbara set the book aside and removed her sunglasses to slip them under the chair out of the sun. She rolled onto her stomach and curved an arm under her head for a pillow. The sun's rays were warm and relaxing and she dozed.

"Didn't anybody ever tell you that you shouldn't sleep in the sun?" Jock's drawling voice wakened her.

She was instantly on the defensive. "I wasn't sleeping." Barbara opened her eyes and was dazzled by the white smile against tanned features, so strongly male and potently handsome. "I was just . . . " she faltered for an explanation.

"Sleeping," Jock supplied knowingly.

He was too devilishly attractive in that mood. Barbara turned her head to face away from him and deny that she was at all disturbed by his latently sensual charm. She even made her voice sound irritated.

"So what if I was sleeping?" she challenged, her words half-mumbled because her cheek was resting on her wrist. She closed her eyes tightly, pretending to ignore him.

"Then you should at least have some lotion on that beautiful skin of yours," he dictated.

Something cold squirted in a squiggly line down her backbone. Barbara yelped at the shock and started to rise, but Jock's hand pushed her back down into her former position. He began smearing the suntan lotion over her back.

"I really don't need this," Barbara protested. "I'm going back into the pool in a few minutes and this will all wash off." She tried to lever halfway up with her elbows.

"Just be quiet and enjoy it." The weight of his hand between her shoulder blades pressed her back down.

It would be much too easy to enjoy it. His hands were gliding over her shoulders and spine with intimate ease. It wasn't just the sun that was warming her flesh. Jock sat down on the edge of the lounge chair and Barbara inched her hip away from the contact with him.

"Don't you have a ranch to run?" she demanded when his hand wandered down to the hollow of her spine, sending crazy, curling sensations all the way down to her toes. "Shouldn't you be off somewhere working?"

"I have been. But I discovered I was hungry and realized I didn't have lunch. Didn't you miss me?" he taunted and began rubbing the lotion on the skin of her waist and hipbones.

"No, I didn't," Barbara lied, and struggled to appear unmoved by the stimulating massage of his hands.

"I was on my way to the house to rob the refrigerator when I saw you sleeping in the sun with all that naked skin exposed, all shiny and golden. You look very delectable lying here. Maybe I should eat you." His mouth opened on her shoulder bone to rake his teeth over its sensitive skin in a sensual bite. Barbara gasped at the shock waves that quaked her and missed feeling his fingers unfasten the back hook of her bikini bra. As soon as she felt the sudden looseness around her chest, she realized what he had done.

"What are you doing?" she demanded angrily and twisted her hands behind her back to try to refasten it.

But while she was doing that, Jock untied the knot at the back of her neck, freeing the top completely.

A sound of angry exasperation came from her throat, tinged with a desperate panic. All the while his hands kept moving and rubbing, purposely interfering with her attempts to refasten the top. Barbara finally gave up the struggle.

"Why did you do that?" Barbara hissed, her voice wavering from her sheer helplessness.

"This suntan lotion will leave a stain on cloth," he reasoned in a vibrantly amused tone. "I didn't want to ruin your swimsuit."

"How thoughtful of you," she murmured sarcastically.

"I thought it was," Jock agreed, not hiding the humor he found in her discomfort.

Without the obstruction of her swimsuit straps, his hands were free to roam every inch of her back. The lotion lubricated her flesh so his hands could glide smoothly and sensuously over her. His manipulating fingers kneaded the taut cords at the base of her neck, rubbing out the tension. Then, working from the base of her spine, his thumbs followed the rippling line of her backbone up to her shoulders where his hands smoothed out to her arms. On the way back to her spine, his hands made a firm exploration of the sides of her rib cage, fingertips brushing the swelling curve of her breasts.

Her fingers curled into the beach towel, crumpling the terry-cloth material into her palms. The teasing brush on her breasts was deliberate. It was meant to get a reaction from her. She steeled herself not to let it show that his intimate touch bothered her, not to take the bait, to pretend that she was indifferent. But each time Jock became bolder and bolder, his fingers exploring more of the full curve.

"Will you stop it?" Barbara choked on the whispered demand.

"Stop what?" Jock feigned ignorance and bent to nibble at her shoulder, sending excited goose bumps over her skin.

At the same time, his hands made a bolder foray, curving to the underside of her breasts. "Stop doing that," she ordered.

"Do you mean this?" His hand slid again toward her breast and Barbara tried to knock it away with her arm.

"Yes!" she hissed, her arm missing altogether.

"Don't you like it?" he mocked. With an ease that revealed his muscled strength, Jock half picked her up and turned her over. The unfastened bikini top ended up beneath her. In panic, Barbara grabbed at his forearms, hard bone and sinew beneath her fingers.

"What are you doing? Someone could see us from the house," Barbara protested in wild desperation. The almost physical touch of his eyes made a slow inspection of her maturely feminine figure.

"No one can see you...unless I move," he pointed out lazily. Which was true. His broad shoulders shielded her from the view of anyone in the house. "Do you want me to move?"

"Yes...no," she retracted quickly.

She didn't know what she wanted him to do, so Jock did what he wanted. "You have a beautiful body, honey, and lovely breasts." He cupped one in his hand. "So very ripe and firm and palely gold, they remind me of grapefruit."

As he bent toward her, Barbara turned her face aside, but Jock didn't seem interested in pursuing her lips, preferring instead the exposed curve of her throat. She moaned at the erotic teasing of his warm breath in her ear as his teeth made love nips on her lobe.

"Jock, stop it," she pleaded. "What if Todd comes back?"

"Is he gone?" he murmured against her neck and worked his way down her throat.

"You know he is," Barbara whispered, trying to be angry, but too many other delirious sensations were crowding in, especially when his mouth continued its downward trek to climb a breast and roll his tongue around a rosy peak.

"Frankly, I didn't give him a thought." Jock kissed the other one to treat them equally and Barbara found that her fingers were digging into the hard flesh of his back, holding him instead of fighting him. Lifting his head, he studied her flushed and aroused face. His gaze lingered on her parted lips, knowing they wanted his kiss. He lowered his mouth closer to tantalize them. "Do you know what Todd would do if he found us like this?"

"No." She didn't want to think about it. She couldn't think about it with his mouth brushing feather-soft against the outline of her lips.

"He would be understanding and forgiving." There was derision in his murmured answer. "He would be understanding toward you because you can't help yourself, and he'd forgive me because I'm not in control of myself around you." Jock seemed to take great pleasure in tormenting her with near kisses. "Do you know what I would do if I found you like this with Todd?"

"No." It was hardly a sound, more like a strangled breath.

"I'd beat him to a pulp for daring to look at you, to touch you the way I am." His voice was a deep rumbling growl. "Because you are mine. I won't share you with anyone, not even my own brother."

He took her mouth with fierce and bruising possession, claiming from it rights that it would grant to no other. Barbara was swept into the tornadic force of savage passion, her senses spinning under the brilliant fury of his kiss. With an exultant moan she surrendered to the wild desire that only Jock could kindle. An arm slipped beneath her to crush her to him, trying to absorb her body into his own. The cotton of his shirt was abrasive against her naked skin. The outline of the cigarette pack in his pocket was imprinted on her breast. The brutal embrace was sweet pain, needs echoing needs that were beyond physical solution.

His anger burned out quickly without resistance to fuel it. An elemental hunger took its place as his mouth began to devour her lips, sampling their softness and tasting their honeyed response. No longer driven to hold her captive, his hands began caressing her again, enjoying the texture of her silken skin, its roundness, its curves, its fevered tremblings. Her own hands were moving over him with joyous familiarity, glorying in the hard muscles of his arms and back, tangling her fingers in his thick, chestnut gold hair.

When his mouth moved from hers to explore her

cheek and the soft sweep of her lashes, Barbara felt his labored breathing, the fiery warmth of his disturbed breath against her skin. She had aroused him fully, and it was a heady knowledge.

"Does Todd make you feel like this?" Jock lifted his head long enough to let his darkly gold eyes blaze possessively over her face. "Do you quiver like hot clay in his arms?"

"No," Barbara admitted. His chin and jaw rubbed against her cheek, the faint stubble of a beard sensually scraping at her skin, as his mouth moved against her temple.

"I want you," he declared huskily. "It doesn't matter whether it's in the gold glare of broad daylight or the velvet blackness of midnight."

The mention of Todd's name had returned a thread of sanity to her delirious mind. "All I am to you is a toy that you discarded and forgot until somebody else picked me up," she said with a bitter, soft laugh. "You don't really want me. You just don't want anyone else to have me."

"That isn't true," Jock dismissed her statement. His hand came up to imprison her face while he moved inches away to glare accusingly. "You want me to make love to you, so don't deny it."

"I don't deny it." There was an ache in her throat that made speech difficult. "But all you have to offer is lust, Jock. A raw, wild passion that's glorious while it lasts."

His jaw hardened. "If lust is all we have, then I'm satisfied with that." His mouth came down to claim hers, but she avoided it.

"It isn't enough for me." Barbara felt the heat of tears in her eyes and willed them not to fall. "I'm more than just a receptacle of animal needs to Todd. He cares about me as a person."

For an instant Jock was motionless. But Barbara could feel the seething anger coiling his muscles and waited for the explosion of temper. She steeled herself against a physical onslaught, but Jock attacked with scathing words.

"You are nothing but an orphan stray that Todd brought home. Yes, he cares about you. He'll care just as much for the stray he brings home next month or next year. If he lost you tomorrow, he wouldn't hurt for long. There are too many strays for him to find and he has enough love for them all." His low voice was laced with scorn.

Barbara guessed that Jock was probably right. It wasn't that Todd's affection was shallow. It was genuine, but easily transferred to the next lost soul that came along.

"With Todd I at least have love," she argued bravely. "Why should I settle for the crust when I can have the whole slice?"

"Is that what you think you're getting from Todd? The whole slice?" The gleam in his tawny eyes was contemptuous.

"Yes." Barbara choked on the whisper.

"You're not. You're just getting the soft, doughy center. You'll never be satisfied with that."

"But he'll make me happier than you can," she retorted in a small, tight voice. "That's the point behind all this, isn't it?"

Jock glared at her for another long minute before he levered away and straightened from the lounge chair, turning his back to her. Wretched with love for him, Barbara watched his fingers coil around the back of his neck. She crossed her arms in front of her to cover herself and hug the pain throbbing inside. As if picking up her silent movement, Jock sliced a glance over his shoulder.

"For God's sake, tidy yourself up!" he snapped.

His anger stung and Barbara rolled away from him onto her stomach. Her fingers were all thumbs as she tried to fit the top to her breasts and fasten the hook behind her back. Jock was watching her and she sensed his impatience with her fumbling efforts. Suddenly his hands were roughly pushing hers out of the way.

"I can do it," she protested against the torture of his touch. Her eyes burned with tears, the heat scorching them dry before they could fall.

"Just shut up." Cold and impersonal, he fastened the back hook and pushed her head down to tie the straps. Barbara suffered a thousand agonies and made not a sound. When he finished, Jock stood up to look down at her prone figure, but she didn't move. "We aren't finished, you and I. Not yet."

It was a warning. Barbara didn't mistake it for anything else as his long strides carried him away from the pool toward the house.

Pushing out of the chair, she walked to the edge of the pool and dove into the cool water. She swam the length of the pool, releasing the frustrated energy born of unsatisfied desires. The ache in the pit of her stomach went away, but not the pain in her heart. It wouldn't be soothed so easily.

There were no drinks before dinner on the veranda that Thursday since dinner was served early. The meal was a light snack to leave room for the food and drinks that would be served at the party after the ranch's riding competition. Barbara lingered at the table, nibbling at a sectioned orange until Jock left the house.

"You are awfully quiet, Barbara," Lillian commented. "What are you thinking about so solemnly?"

"I . . . was just trying to decide whether I should wear slacks or a dress tonight," she lied. She had no taste for the juicy flesh of the orange and set it aside.

"That depends," Todd inserted, "on whether you want to ride over to the arena or take a car. Which would you like to do?"

"I think I'd rather ride." Barbara opted for the transportation that would demand the least amount of conversation.

"Then you'd better go change so we can start out," he suggested, "while I arrange to have the horses saddled and brought to the house."

In her room, Barbara put on a pair of bone-colored denims and a blue madras blouse.

When she came downstairs Todd was waiting for her. He, too, had changed into more rugged clothing for the ride. The horses were outside. It was an older man who handed Barbara the reins to the blaze-faced chestnut.

"Where was Mike?" she asked Todd after they

had mounted and started the horses down the lane.

"At the arena already, I imagine."

The rhythmic gait of the horse beneath her and Todd's easy company were letting Barbara relax. "How long will this last—the competition, I mean?"

"Until the sun goes down. Eight, eight-thirty."

"Is it like a rodeo?" she questioned.

"Do you mean bucking broncos and bull riding?" Todd smiled. "No. It's mostly roping and cutting cattle. Once in a while there is a young horse that's kinda rank and the boys will take their turns on it, but that's an exception rather than the rule."

There was a confusion of trucks and horse trailers when they arrived at the arena grounds. Horses and riders were milling about, some in the arena and others weaving through the congestion of parked vehicles and people. Most of the men that worked on Sandoval were married. Their wives and families had come along with them to watch the competition. Since there weren't any bleachers to sit in, many of the women had brought folding lawn chairs to set outside the white-railed fence of the arena, close to the end where the chutes were.

Their arrival didn't go unnoticed. As Todd led the way to the trailer where they were going to leave their horses tied, greetings were called out all along the way. A few of the people Barbara had already met, but most of them she hadn't seen so there was a constant stream of introductions as she and Todd rode their horses to the trailer and walked back to the arena fence.

"Do you have the feeling you've just run the gauntlet?" Todd laughed softly, putting an arm around her waist as they both leaned on the top rail.

"Yes," she admitted. At the far end of the arena, she saw a muscled, iron-gray horse that she instantly recognized as Jock's. He was sitting casually in the saddle, talking to another cowboy. "Will Jock be competing in any of the events tonight?" Barbara asked, trying to sound casual even though her heart was knocking against her ribs.

"No, he hasn't been riding in them for the last few years. Usually he takes part in the judging."

"Why hasn't he been riding?" curiosity made her ask.

"Because he was winning all the time," Todd grinned. "Well, not all of the time," he conceded, "but a lot. J.R. is quite a competitor and he loves to win. Being the owner, he didn't think it was right so he quit riding."

"I see," she murmured, but she was thinking about that reference to Jock as a competitor and his desire to win. Jock had warned her that he hadn't given up. Barbara glanced at the diamond sparkling in the sunlight. It wasn't much of a defense anymore. And neither was Todd, although she still felt safe when she was with him.

"They're clearing the arena," Todd observed. "It looks like they are going to start with calf roping first."

The horses and riders began filing out of the arena through the gate near where Todd and Barbara were standing. A hefty-sized calf was prodded along the chutes while the first roper backed his horse into the box beside the chute. Jock and another rider stayed in the arena to judge and time the event.

It was impossible for Barbara to watch each of the contestants without being aware of the rider on the big gray horse. When the calf roping was over, Mike Turbot had won the event. The fact that it was someone she knew made it more interesting to Barbara.

"Congratulations, Mike," she called to him when he rode past.

"Thanks." He reined his horse to a stop and modestly insisted, "Half the guys out there could beat me."

"But they didn't," Barbara pointed out.

"Yeah, well—" Mike shrugged, looking pleased "—all these events require skills that a cowboy and his horse have to have to work on a ranch. Like roping a calf for branding and like this next event, cutting a steer out from a herd. These are things you've got to do every day."

"You are good at it."

"So are the others. You should see them in action for real. As a matter of fact, they're going to be rounding up the spring calves over in the Crosstimber section. You should have Jock take you over there one day to watch. It's interesting if you've never seen one before," Mike suggested.

"I'll bet it would be." But Barbara doubted that she would ask Jock.

Mike glance toward the arena and edged his horse toward the fence. "Hey, Jock!" he called him to the fence.

Jock trotted the gray toward the fence. Barbara felt his gaze touch her and flick to Todd before centering on Mike. "What is it, Mike?" he asked with seeming casualness.

"Vince dislocated his shoulder and can't ride in the team roping with me," Mike explaned, and Barbara experienced a twinge of relief that he hadn't suggested Jock take her to see the roundup. "I wondered if you would be my partner."

"I'll see if I can't get someone to take over as timer for me on that event," Jock agreed after a brief hesitation.

"Great. Let me know," Mike nodded.

"I will." Jock let his gaze slide to Barbara. "Are you enjoying yourself?"

"Yes." She felt wary.

Todd spoke up. "Mike was just mentioning that you'd be rounding up calves over at Crosstimber."

"Yes, starting Monday," Jock admitted.

"I think Barbara would find it fascinating to watch," Todd explained.

"Yes." Jock gave her a considering look, his mouth twitching in what might have been a dry smile. "I'll see about making arrangements for you to come on Tuesday. Would that be all right?"

"If it's all right with Todd." Barbara shrugged, not endorsing the date nor the idea.

"Tuesday will be fine," Todd agreed. "You'd like to go, wouldn't you, Barbara?"

"Of course," she said because it was expected of her.

"Hey, Jock!" The other man who had been acting

as judge with him waved to him. ''They are ready to start the cutting competition.''

''See you later.'' The encompassing phrase was issued before Jock pivoted the gray horse away from the rail.

CHAPTER SEVEN

BEFORE THE TEAM ROPING STARTED, Jock rode out of the arena and another man took his place to judge the event. As she realized that he would be competing, Barbara's interest in the event was increased. When the first team of two ropers entered the arena, she turned to Todd.

"What is the purpose of this event? Its practical use in ranching?" she questioned. "Why would a cowboy have to rope a full-grown steer? Obviously it would already have been branded as a calf?"

"Generally it's done to treat an injured or sick animal. Sometimes it's referred to as 'heading and heeling' because one rider ropes the horns or the cow's head and the second rider catches the hind feet in his loop. The steer is stretched between them till he goes down so he can be treated," Todd explained.

The first pair of ropers in the event ended up with no time when the second roper failed to catch the hind legs. "It's tricky," was Todd's comment.

When Mike Turbot and Jock rode into the arena, Barbara could feel the change in the atmosphere. There was more than ordinary interest from the onlookers who worked for the man about to compete.

The big gray horse seemed aware of the change, too. It sidestepped into the arena, almost galloping in place, its neck arched, all coiled speed waiting to be released.

The steer was in the chute. Jock backed the gray into the boxed opening on the right of the chute and Mike put his horse in the left. The chute gate sprang up, releasing the steer. The animal had a length's head start before the two riders bounded after it. Within two strides, Mike was swinging his lariat and tossing it over the steer's horns. He dallied the rope around his saddle horn, turning his horse and pulling the steer around to offer the hindquarters to Jock's rope. His loop snaked low to the ground and was jerked tight above the steer's hind hooves. In the blink of an eye the steer was on the ground, the ropes taut on either side. The time was lightning fast.

There was no applause as the two men rode out of the arena. A couple of people shouted their approval. But there was a look Barbara noticed in the eyes of the cowboys, a gleam of respect when they glanced at their boss.

"Great job. You've done it again, J.R." There wasn't a trace of envy in Todd's voice as he congratulated his brother. "I'll make a side bet with you that you just posted the winning time."

"I won't bet," Jock refused, but inner satisfaction was written in his features. The gray horse tossed its head, rolling out a snort, as it paused near Todd and Barbara.

Mike stopped alongside of him. "You had that

loop around the steer's hind feet before I even had it turned properly. That was some roping, boss.''

"Give some credit to Ghost." Jock patted the arched neck of his horse. "He put me in position to make the throw."

"Yeah, and you trained him," Mike stated and moved off with a wry shake of his head. "A good horse just makes a good cowboy look even better."

The praise seemed to tighten Jock's features. Barbara sensed he didn't like it whether it was earned or not. It made him uncomfortable, because of his position as owner, she supposed. Jock's finger touched his hat before he pivoted the gray horse toward the collection of horse trailers.

Another team of ropers entered the arena and Barbara turned absently to watch them. But her mind was on the man astride the gray horse. Even when she was determined not to think about him, she did.

Before the event was over, Todd asked, "Did you want to ride the horses back? I can borrow Ramon's truck if you want to go back to the house and change before everyone arrives for the party."

"What about the horses?" she inquired with a frown.

"We can send them back in one of the horse trailers. Mike will look after them. If we ride them, it will take longer."

He seemed to think that was a concern. Barbara wasn't looking forward to the engagement party all that eagerly. She didn't object to being late, but obviously Todd did.

"Maybe you should ask Ramon if we could use his truck, then," she said.

"Wait here while I find him." He pressed a kiss to her temple before leaving.

Barbara turned back to watch the rest of the team-roping event. Mike and Jock were the winners when all the times were in. Todd still hadn't come back for her when the next event started. When Mike rode by, Barbara stopped him.

"Have you seen Todd?"

"Yeah, he was over by Ramon's pickup." Mike pointed. "It's that blue one behind the red and white horse trailer."

"I see it. Thanks." She started off toward it.

She had to zigzag around trucks and trailers, dodging horses and riders along the way. It was an obstacle course, she decided when she stopped to let one horse pass in front of her while another walked behind her. Intent on avoiding what was ahead of her, Barbara didn't notice the gray horse approaching from behind.

"Todd is looking for you," Jock announced, causing Barbara to start in surprise.

"Where is he?" Her glance ricocheted from his mocking features to search the crowd of faces. "He went to borrow Ramon's truck so we could leave and I—" The gray horse was maneuvered in front of her to block her path.

"Hop on and I'll take you to him." Jock stretched an arm down to help her swing into the saddle behind him.

She didn't want to be that close to him. "No, thanks. I'll walk. Just tell me where Todd is."

"He's over by Ramon's truck, but it will be easier—and safer—to ride. There are a lot of horses, hooves to dodge."

But Barbara ignored his suggestion and ducked under the muscled neck of the gray horse to continue in the direction of the blue pickup. She had taken three steps when an arm hooked her waist and she was scooped off the ground. Barbara struggled angrily as Jock sat her on the front of the saddle.

"Put me down, you big ape!" she ordered, unaware of how loud her voice was until she heard two cowboys chuckling.

"Got trouble, boss?" one called.

And Barbara crimsoned, flashing a resentful glance at Jock's mocking countenance so close to her own. His arm circled her waist so tightly that her shoulder was wedged against the unyielding wall of his chest. There was a smile on his mouth but not in his eyes.

"How about this, boys?" he responded to their comment. "I come riding up on an almost white horse and plan to carry off a beautiful lady into the night — and this is what happens."

"You take me to Todd," she hissed.

"I said I would," Jock reminded her in a voice as low as hers had been.

She felt the gray horse bunch its muscled hindquarters at the touch of Jock's heel. It gave a little jump forward before a check of the reins slowed

it to a quick-stepping walk. Barbara held herself
rigid in Jock's tight hold. But she wasn't in a position
to balance herself and had to rely on his support to
keep her on the horse. She forced her gaze to the
front, looking for Todd, but with each breath she
took, her senses were filled with drugging scents of
Jock, spicy and male. She almost didn't see Todd
standing beside the blue truck.

"There you are." Todd walked forward when
Jock stopped the horse and lifted Barbara from the
saddle. "Thanks, J.R."

"See you at the house." The silent promise of that
statement was in the look he let linger on Barbara
before turning the big gray gelding away from the
truck.

Barbara tried to pretend that the look held no
significance and turned to Todd. "What was the
problem?"

"What problem?" His expression was blank.

"I waited for you, but you didn't come back."

"No, I sent J.R. to get you. It was a lot safer on
horseback to get through this jam of horses and
trailers. Weren't you at the gate when he found
you?" Todd asked.

"No, I'd come looking for you. I didn't realize
you had sent Jock for me," Barbara said with a trace
of irritation.

Todd opened the passenger door of the truck cab
for her "Why? Does it matter?"

"I just wish you hadn't sent Jock for me, that's
all," she said impatiently.

"He hasn't been bothering you lately, has he?" Todd frowned.

Only when you aren't around. But she didn't say that. "I just wish you hadn't sent him, that's all," she repeated.

Todd walked around the front of the truck and slid behind the wheel. "You might as well get used to his being around, Barbara," he said firmly. "You'll see a lot of him once we're married."

"Not if Jock has his way," she murmured.

"His way about what? Seeing us or getting married?"

"Either one." Barbara shrugged, not wanting to continue the conversation, and Todd let it drop.

The truck made the drive to the main house seem relatively short. The sky was golden with a lingering sunset when Todd stopped in front of the hacienda-style building. Climbing out of the cab unassisted, Barbara hurried into the courtyard. Through the arched openings leading to the veranda she saw Lillian Gaynor setting a platter on a buffet table that had been set up to hold the food. The woman glanced up at the sound of Barbara's footsteps in the courtyard.

"You're back. How was the competition? Did you enjoy it?"

"Yes, it was fun," Barbara replied. "I'm going upstairs to wash off this arena dust and change clothes, then I'll be down to help you."

"Don't rush. Antonia and I have just about everything done. Besides, this is the groom's party. The prospective bride doesn't have to worry about all the refreshments. So take your time," Lillian insisted, then added, "Oh, dress casually. Most everyone will come as they are from the arena."

"Okay. Thanks for the warning." Barbara hurried toward the double-door entrance to the foyer, and its stairwell.

While she was in her room washing and changing, she heard the sounds of trucks and cars driving up, doors slamming, and a multitude of voices congregating on the veranda. Taking Lillian's advice, Barbara changed into a simple white peasant blouse, pulling the elasticized neckline over her shoulders and wearing a plain wraparound skirt of red cotton with it.

The party seemed to be in full swing when she stepped onto the veranda. Built-in speakers piped music outside from the entertainment center in the house. The guests were all talking and laughing with either a plate of food in their hands or a beer. Todd appeared almost instantly at her side to take her in hand.

"Are you hungry?" He led her toward the buffet table, mounded with platters of sandwiches, cheeses, fruits, hot hors d'oeuvres and chips.

"Not very." She shook her head.

"Want something to drink? We have a couple of kegs of beer and some punch. I have to warn you somebody spiked the punch very generously. If you drink any of it, be warned," he chuckled.

"No iced tea, I suppose," Barbara said with a mock sigh.

"Hey, this is supposed to be a celebration," he chided her playfully. "Some punch for the lady," he ordered and Barbara found a glass cup being forced into her hand. Todd bent toward her and whispered again, "Be warned."

She took a tentative sip and felt the fire in her throat. "It is strong," she agreed, unable to stop a coughing protest.

"You can carry it around with you all night. No one will notice if you don't drink it." Todd grinned and linked his arm in hers. "Come on. I think we'd better circulate. This is a friendly group. I don't know what you've heard about cowboys, but this bunch loves to dance. Most of them are pretty good so you won't have to worry about smashed toes."

Todd's information proved to be correct on all counts. It was a very friendly and open crowd. Barbara found it easy to talk and laugh with them. No one noticed that all she did was moisten her lips with the potent drink in her glass cup without the liquid ever depreciating any great amount. Mike Turbot was the first to come up and ask her to dance. When she proved to be a willing partner, it seemed to break the ice and she was inundated with invitations.

Slow dances, fast dances and the in-between tempos—she danced them all. Her partners were young cowboys, old ones and middle-aged. Barbara was half-convinced that every man at the party was determined to dance with Todd's future bride. It became impossible to refuse anyone for fear of offending him. Besides, Barbara couldn't remember the last time she had danced so much, and she was having fun.

The song ended and she thanked her partner, a young fresh-faced cowboy whose name she couldn't remember. As she paused for a breath while the record changed, a hand tapped her shoulder. Barbara turned with a start, half expecting to find Jock confronting her. She had seen him on the fringes of several groups all evening but so far hadn't encountered him.

"Ramon," she laughed in relief.

"If the next song is a slow one, may I have this dance?" he asked with a formal little bow. "I don't have the wind anymore for the faster songs."

"I would be delighted," Barbara agreed with a slight curtsy.

A hand gripped the curve of her waist from behind. "Sorry, Ramon," Jock said without apology. "But I'm claiming a prior right to this dance." He was already turning her into his arms as he spoke.

"Oh, but—" Barbara tried to protest, looking frantically over her shoulder at Ramon.

"It is all right. I will wait until later," he assured her and turned away.

With that excuse gone, Barbara had to seek hurriedly for another. At the same time, she made the discomfiting discovery that Jock had both arms around her waist, his large hands splayed over the small of her back. She had no place for her own hands but his chest, and the lower half of her body was being molded to his.

"I'd really rather sit this dance out," she said nervously, staring at the buttons on his shirt.

"Would you? Why?" His drawling tone indicated that he knew the reason: he disturbed her too much.

"I'm tired. I've been dancing practically every dance. I'd like to catch my breath." It sounded reasonable to Barbara.

"You were willing enough to dance when Ramon asked you," Jock reminded her with infuriating mockery, knowing it was a vital point she had overlooked in her search for an excuse. "Since you are tired, we won't move around too much. You are free to lean on me if your feet hurt."

"No, thank you." The stilted little refusal sounded ridiculous even to her own ears, so prudishly silly and absurd.

The way their bodies were swaying together, so exactly in unison with each other and the tempo of the slow music, sounded more alarm bells in her head. She flattened her hands against his chest, trying to wedge more space between them, but her action only curved her hips more fully against the rippling muscles in his thighs. Although they were barely moving, Barbara discovered that they were in the more shadowed area of the veranda, away from the lanterns strung near the buffet tables. She stopped straining away from his chest since it was only creating a worse disturbance. The warmth of his breath stirred her hair.

"With all that creamy skin in view, I'm surprised somebody hasn't taken a bite out of you," Jock murmured and bent his head toward a bare shoulder. "I'm surprised they could resist."

Barbara wiggled in protest, but she couldn't stop him from nibbling at the base of her neck. "Not everyone is as cannibalistic as you are, Jock." She tried to sound angry, but it was difficult with a quiver of excitement racing over her skin.

"They don't know what they're missing." His firm lips formed the words against her neck, continuing his exploration with bold unconcern.

"Jock, stop it." Barbara squirmed uncomfortably, liking what he was doing and afraid of it at the same time. "Somebody might see you. What would they think?"

"That I'm making time with my brother's fiancée," he laughed softly against her skin. "Which is precisely what I'm doing. But keep pretending to struggle and they'll think you are just trying to avoid an embarrassing scene."

He nipped at her earlobe and Barbara shuddered against him. "Don't do this, please."

With a sudden, twisting turn, Jock maneuvered her behind an arch where curious eyes couldn't see them. He leaned against the concrete support, pulled her hard into his arms and covered her lips with a hungry, burning kiss. It happened so fast Barbara had no warning and her response was purely instinctive. Her hands glided around his neck while he pressed her malleable form to the hard contours of his length. It was a wild, crazy insanity that claimed them both, but Barbara thrilled to it.

Until Lillian's voice gasped a shocked, "Jock, what are you doing?"

The demand ripped the kiss apart. Too shaken to move, Barbara hid her reddening face in Jock's shadow, averted from the gentle woman she had grown to like. Her fingers were slow to unclasp themselves from around his neck, like child's hands guiltily inching away from a cookie jar.

"You missed the point, mother," Jock said, drawing a deep breath. "What is Barbara doing to stop me?"

Her humiliation was complete. It only needed Jock to set her away from him and leave, which he did. Barbara stood defenseless in front of his mother, too ashamed to speak and too embarrassed to move. The weighted silence stretched for several seconds. Then Lillian stepped toward her and curved a hand around Barbara's bare shoulders, which had only moments ago been warmed by Jock's mouth.

"Come with me, dear," Lillian murmured. "We both need a few moments to collect ourselves."

"Thank you. Yes." Her voice was shaking as badly as her nerves were. She couldn't have faced that happy, laughing crowd just on the other side of the arch.

Lillian guided her through a side entrance into the house, away from the noise of the party. Once the doors were shut and they were alone, the woman's brown eyes made a quick inspection of Barbara's pale complexion.

"Would you like a drink? A brandy, perhaps?" she suggested.

"No. No, thank you," Barbara refused with a quick shake of her head. She moistened her lips nervously, knowing there were going to be questions.

"I'm sure this isn't any of my business," Lillian began with a sigh. "But as a mother to both Todd and Jock, I can't exactly be called a disinterested party."

"I know. I'm sorry." Barbara swallowed.

"I know that you and Jock had met before. But I had the impression that despite the interest he expressed in you, you were no longer interested in him. That obviously isn't the case, is it?"

"I—" Barbara stopped and admitted, "No, that isn't the case."

"Are you in love with Todd? Or Jock?"

"Both." Barbara realized that answer demanded more of an explanation. "In different ways. Todd makes me feel so safe and protected. Jock takes me to the edge of the world." She rubbed her arms, fighting a chill.

"How well did you know Jock?" Lillian phrased the question delicately.

Barbara took a deep breath and released it in a sigh. "Very well."

There was a long pause before she asked, "What happened between you?"

"It just didn't work out." Barbara shrugged, not wanting to go into that long story again. She felt the sting of tears in her eyes. "But he isn't going to make me cry again. I'm not going to let him," she protested in a voice that sounded amazingly calm and rational.

"How much of this have you told Todd?"

"All of it. He's aware that I still find Jock very attractive, physically." Barbara twisted the diamond ring on her finger. "Todd has suggested that I take these two weeks to make up my mind whether we should be married. So far I haven't been very successful at treating Jock like a brother." She smiled bitterly.

"I think Todd made a very sensible suggestion. Engagements are meant to be a sort of trial period."

"What would you do, Lillian?" Barbara lifted her gaze, her blue eyes dark and haunted with uncertainty.

"That isn't a fair question." She laughed briefly in surprise. "I hope that I would do what I felt in my heart was right."

"Yes, of course." She turned away, a little dispirited.

"That isn't an adequate answer, I know," Lillian murmured. "It must be very difficult for you. But I don't trust myself to be sufficiently impartial to give you more specific advice."

"You have been very understanding as it is." Barbara meant that very sincerely. "I wouldn't blame you if you didn't want me for a daughter-in-law. I certainly haven't made a very good impression, considering my behavior tonight."

"I was young once," Lillian reminded her. "It

may be hard to believe, but it's true.'' Her brown eyes held a gently twinkling light.

Barbara smiled. ''I find it very easy to believe, because you are still very young in many ways.''

''Now you have made an excellent impression.'' Lillian laughed with a soft warmth.

''I meant it,'' Barbara insisted, not wanting the woman to think she was attempting to flatter her. ''I didn't say it just to—''

''I know you didn't,'' Lillian assured her quickly. ''If you feel up to it, we should return to the party before our guests begin speculating on the cause of our absence.''

Barbara wished there was a way she didn't have to return at all, which, of course, was impossible. Thanks to the older woman's quiet understanding, her nerves were in better shape, although she wasn't certain how much her shattered poise could withstand.

''Yes. Todd will be wondering where I am,'' she agreed with the suggestion.

Exiting the house through the veranda doors, Barbara was immediately enveloped in the noise of the party. The music and laughing voices hammered at her ears. Lillian paused beside her while Barbara searched the crowd of faces. Someone called to Lillian and she excused herself to resume her duties as hostess. At almost the same moment, Barbara saw Todd separate himself from a small group and walk toward her.

''I've been looking for you,'' he accused gently

and took her hand to pull her to his side. "The last time I saw you, you were dancing with J.R. Then you simply disappeared. Where were you? Powdering your nose?" He kissed the side of her hair, nestling her inside the crook of his arm.

Todd offered her the perfect excuse, but honesty wouldn't permit her to take it. "Your mother and I were talking." She paused a pulse beat. "She rescued me from Jock."

He was still for an instant, every muscle tensed. Barbara lifted her gaze to his face and found him staring at a distant point. She glanced in the same direction.

Jock was standing by the punch bowl, looking back at the two of them. His hard gaze fell as he partially turned his head. A muscle flexed in his cheek from a sudden clenching of his jaw; then he was downing the contents of a glass and turning to ladle more punch into it.

"Let's dance." Todd didn't give her a chance to refuse as he escorted her to the area of the veranda where other couples were swaying to the music coming from the speaker system.

Held close in his arms, Barbara felt gently protected. Todd's undemanding embrace was a haven for her storm-tossed emotions. She relaxed under his comforting hold, no longer needing to be on guard against harm.

"Is he getting to you?" Todd murmured near her ear.

Barbara released a long sigh. "Jock always could.

I think you made a mistake when you brought this stray home, Todd.''

'Mmm.'' he made the negative sound against her hair. "I couldn't let you keep wandering around so lost and alone. You need someone to look after you.''

Was that what she needed? Once Barbara had thought she just wanted someone to care about her. Now she wasn't so sure. Her glance strayed to the punch bowl. Jock was still there, the glass cup in his hand, watching them with hard amber eyes.

CHAPTER EIGHT

Around midnight the party began to wear itself out. A few had already gone home. Although the rest still lingered, their voices were subdued and the music quieter. They had separated into groups without much mingling going on between them. Barbara knew the party was on the verge of breaking up, and she was glad.

"Mother has brought out some coffee. Would you like some?" Todd asked.

Barbara glanced to see Lillian setting a coffee service on the buffet table. For once, Jock wasn't in the vicinity of the punch bowl, a place he had haunted since their dance. She looked back at Todd, her bulwark that evening.

"Yes, coffee would be great," she agreed and he led her to the table.

As he started to pour them each a cup of coffee, Ramon and Connie Morales approached them. "We are leaving now," Ramon announced. "We wished to say goodbye."

"I'm glad you came, both of you." Barbara's smile was stiff from being forced on her face all evening.

"We enjoyed ourselves," Connie declared.

"We never did have our dance, did we, Ramon?" Barbara remembered, and voiced it unconsciously.

"You did not seem in the mood to dance later," he replied. Did his dark gaze linger on her a little too wisely before he turned to Todd? "Barbara is a lovely woman. You must be proud of her, Todd."

"I am," he stated. "And I have already discovered how lovely she is."

"Wrong, little brother." With animal quietness, Jock appeared at her side. His hand hooked her waist to pull her against his hip. "I discovered her first. That means she belongs to me." There was a possessive ring in his voice that carried over the veranda, silencing conversations.

The hard imprint of his length burned down her side. The onslaught of heat made her weak and shaky inside, but the awareness of curious eyes watching gave Barbara the strength to struggle. She pushed at his hard stomach.

"You're making a scene, Jock," she protested.

"Why? Do you think they haven't noticed that I haven't been able to take my eyes off you all evening? Or the way you kept looking for me? You are mine, regardless of what that ring on your finger is supposed to represent," he jeered.

His warm breath washed her face with a potent mixture of fruit and alcohol. "You're drunk," Barbara accused in a hopeless attempt to negate his statement.

"Am I?" Keeping an arm around her, Jock placed a hand along the side of her neck, jamming his thumb under the point of her chin and forcing it up. The pressure of his grip was barely controlled. "Drinking is supposed to dull the senses. So why am I so keenly aware of the fragrance of your hair, the taste of your breath and the feel of your body against mine?"

Denied the ability to swallow or speak, Barbara couldn't reply. The hand at the back of her waist made a sensual exploration of her lower spine.

Jock went on, "If I were stone-cold sober, I'd still want to carry you off into the night the way I—"

"J.R.—" Stepping forward, Todd laid an admonishing hand on his brother's forearm to loose the fingers that gripped Barbara's throat.

In a shrugging movement, Jock released his grip and attempted to knock away Todd's restraining hand, but his swinging arm accidentally struck Todd's chin, drawing a muffled sound of surprise and unconscious pain. Todd rubbed his chin, a stunned frown creasing his forehead as he stared at Jock.

"Todd, I—" Jock's taut voice seemed to come from some deep cavernous well within him, tortured and angry.

"It's all right. It was just an accident," Todd denied the need to apologize.

White-lipped, Jock stared at him for another second before pivoting and leaving the veranda with long, reaching strides. Barbara's hand was at her throat where his hand had been, feeling the identation his digging fingers had left behind and attempting to ease the pain they had left. She watched Jock enter the house, slamming the glass-paned door so that it rattled. Todd moved to her side.

"Are you all right?" She looked up, filled with blame for what happened.

"It didn't hurt," Todd insisted, taking his hand away from his chin. "Not that much. It just surprised me, that's all."

A movement in her side vision reminded Barbara of the presence of Ramon and Connie Morales. She turned, apologizingly guiltily, "I'm sorry this happened. I—"

"It was inevitable," Ramon responded, smiling gently. "It is sad when two brothers fall in love with the same woman."

Love? Barbara questioned that in her mind, but she said nothing.

"Don't feel badly," Connie offered. "Everyone regrets that this happened, including Jock. It's best forgotten."

"Yes," Ramon agreed. "This time we will say good-night."

The departure of the older couple began a general exodus of all the other guests. Barbara stayed at Todd's side to bid them all good-night, but she was just as anxious to leave the veranda as they were.

When they were alone, Todd put an arm around her and suggested, "We never did have our coffee. Would you like that cup now? We can sit down and unwind for a while. In one way or another, it's been a trying evening. You could do with some relaxing."

"I think I'll pass on the coffee," Barbara refused. "I'd rather go to my room. I—"

"You don't have to explain," Todd interrupted and kissed the corner of her mouth. "You'd rather be alone. I can understand that."

"This was supposed to be our engagement party and your fiancée is running off to hide the instant the last guest leaves," Barbara sighed. "Maybe we should call this whole thing off, Todd. This can't be the way you wanted it."

"It isn't, but I have a lot of patience. Good night." He gave her an affectionate push toward the glass-paned doors.

"Aren't you coming?" Barbara paused.

"Not right away." He shook his head and moved to the buffet table.

Barbara watched him pour a cup of coffee from the insulated service, then turned to enter the house. Passing through the informal family room, she walked into the hall that led to the foyer. It took her past the door to a small den. Usually the door was closed. This time it was standing open. Her gaze was drawn into the room.

Jock was reclining in a wooden-armed chair, his long legs stretched out in front of him. An empty glass was in his hand, and his hair was rumpled as if by raking fingers. While Barbara watched with helpless compulsion, Jock partially turned away from the door to reach for something on a table beside him.

As he squared around in the chair, she saw a whiskey bottle in his hand. He started to tip the bottle to fill the glass; then an unpleasant smile pulled at his mouth. Instead of filling the glass, Jock set it aside and took a swig straight from the bottle.

Not conscious of making a sound, Barbara nonetheless became the object of his slicing gaze. His features seemed to harden into bronze, smooth and emotionless except for topaz flames in his brown

eyes. Uncoiling from the chair, he strode toward the
door, and Barbara took a step backward. His mouth
slanted in harsh mockery as he reached out and
slammed the door shut in her face.

Shaken, she turned away to move to the stairwell
in the foyer. His action made her feel all the more to
blame for what had happened that night. Sleeping
wasn't easy.

IT WAS PAST MIDMORNING when Barbara came down
the stairs. The few hours of sleep she had got had not
left her feeling rested. The party was a perfect excuse
for having slept so late, but Barbara knew Todd had
probably been up earlier—and Jock, too. Everyone
in the household except herself. Which meant if she
had breakfast, it would be alone. Sighing, she turned
into the living room, using it as a shortcut to the
dining room where she knew a pot of coffee would be
warming.

As she started toward the archway, she heard
Jock's voice raised in anger. "I'm too old to be
slapped on the hand, mother. Just stay out of it!"
Lillian murmured a response that Barbara couldn't
hear, but Jock's reply was plain. "I don't need you to
tell me what is right and proper. And for God's sake
quit shouting!"

Barbara hesitated a minute. When she heard the
door leading from the dining room to the kitchen
open and close, she presumed Jock had left and she
started forward again. At least she would be able to
have a cup of coffee with Lillian.

As she rounded the archway, Barbara saw Jock,

not Lillian, seated at the table. His elbows were resting on the polished surface, his forehead cradled in his hands. He was wearing the same clothes he'd had on the previous night. Which indicated to Barbara that he'd slept in them, probably passing out in the den.

A hand that had been shielding his eyes came down to circle a tall glass on the table in front of him. His gaze swept up to stab at Barbara.

"Quit hovering in the doorway," he grumbled. "Come in and have your breakfast. That's what you were going to do, wasn't it?"

"I thought Lillian was here." Barbara hesitated a fraction of a second longer before entering the room and walking to the coffee service.

"She's in the kitchen." Jock didn't move from his position. His mouth twitched cynically as Barbara walked to the table with her coffee. "You'll have to settle for my company." The chair leg scraped the tile floor as she pulled it out, and Jock winced. "Be a little more quiet, please."

"Hangover?" Barbara commented a trifle maliciously.

"It seems a mild description," she sighed.

"What's that?" She glanced at the glass in front of him. The contents reminded her of tomato juice, but the liquid was much too frothy.

"A bit of the hair of the dog that bit me." He took a swallow from it and grimaced. "It's a concoction of Antonia's. I don't know what's in it, and I think I'm better off not knowing. It works, which is what counts."

Sitting opposite him, Barbara didn't find Jock quite so dangerous this morning, despite his obvious ill temper. "Did you just get up?"

"I came to a few minutes ago, which is what you were really asking." His upper lip curled sarcastically. She heard the scrape of day-old bristle as he rubbed his cheek.

"My, but you are touchy this morning." Barbara discovered that she was gloating a bit over his physical suffering. She had gone through enough mental agony over him to find satisfaction in his pain. "Didn't the bottle help you forget?"

The gibe drew his sharp glance, brown eyes shot with glittering sparks of gold. "It helped me forget I accidentally hit my own brother." Jock took a big swallow from the glass while Barbara uncomfortably studied the steam rising from her hot coffee. "Todd has already forgiven me for that." His voice was laced with cold amusement.

"It was an accident. You didn't intend to hit him," she murmured.

"No, I didn't intend to, but if it had been reversed, I would have slugged him on general principles. But not Todd." Jock paused, drawing a deep breath. "He's forgotten. And thanks to my old friend Jack Daniels, so have I."

Barbara sipped at her coffee, blue eyes studying him over the rim of her cup. Strong, sun-browned fingers were massaging a point in the center of his forehead. She suspected that his head was pounding with a thousand sledgehammers. He had to be feeling very rocky.

"Drinking doesn't solve anything, Jock," she commented.

"No, it didn't put you out of my mind," he agreed, lifting his gaze to lock it to hers. "In fact, it only made the memories sharper."

His remark triggered a whole flood of memories to drown Barbara in a time when Jock's nearness had meant ecstatic bliss. She struggled to the surface, breaking free of his gaze to clutch the handle of her coffee cup more tightly.

"Then maybe you shouldn't drink so much," she suggested stiffly.

"More lectures?" His tone was dryly sardonic. "This must be my morning for them. First mother, now you."

She recalled his voice raised in anger at Lillian before she had entered the dining room. "I'm sure Lillian was simply voicing her concern over the way you abused yourself with that liquor bottle last night."

"Oh, she wasn't lecturing me on drinking," Jock corrected her with harsh amusement. "She was accusing me of taking unfair advantage of a previous relationship with you."

Her nerves tingled at the static electricity that suddenly seemed to fill the air. Her gaze roamed the table, looking everywhere but at him. Trying to hide her sudden discomposure, Barbara took another sip of her coffee.

"Well, you are." She forced out a calm answer.

"You don't have to like it." His voice was low and tauntingly seductive. "But the way you respond tells me you do."

An insidious fire licked through her veins. It was impossible to deny his statement, especially when the husky caress of his voice was unnerving her. But Barbara couldn't permit the remark to stand unchallenged.

"People can like something that is no good for them," she defended herself, flicking him a wary look. "Letting you make love to me is a habit, a bad one. It's like lighting up a cigarette without wanting one. You are like a smoking habit to me. A smoker knows cigarettes are bad for his health, but it doesn't stop him from craving one. Only I'm kicking the habit, Jock. I may be suffering withdrawal symptoms, but I'll get over you."

His gaze roamed over her face, pensive and measuring. "Will you? I happen to be incurably addicted. You have me hooked, honey."

It was a heady thought, one that made her reel with the possibilities of tomorrow. But it was an illusion, a mirage. Jock sounded so convincing, but Barbara had evidence it wasn't true.

"Six months, Jock," she reminded him. "You went six months without me. And I can't see where you suffered any ill effects. You can get along without me just fine."

"What makes you think I have?" he challenged dryly.

"It's obvious, isn't it?" Barbara countered. He hadn't made a single attempt to contact her in all that time. He'd never be able to convince her that she meant as much to him as he was attempting to claim. "When we said goodbye, it was final. And I've got along without you very well. So did you. Let's keep it that way."

Her control was splintering. Barbara knew she had to escape before he came up with some new argument to undermine her poise. She pushed her chair away from the table.

"If you'll excuse me, I'm going out to the kitchen to persuade Antonia to fix me some breakfast."

"You aren't going to marry Todd," Jock announced.

Barbara paused at the door to the kitchen. "That is my decision to make, not yours."

"Then I'm going to do my damnedest to be certain you make the right one." His low threat followed her through the door.

DURING THE NEXT TWO DAYS Jock didn't make any overt attempt to carry out his threat. In fact, he seemed to make it a point to stay well clear of her. Barbara wondered whether he was engaging in psychological warfare, letting her fret and stew over what his next move might be. And she did a lot of mental pacing.

Sunday brought another visit to the rural church the family regularly attended. This time Jock went with them. Barbara found herself sandwiched between Jock and Todd, with Lillian sitting on the other side of Jock. The church pews were crowded, making contact with Jock impossible to avoid. Her shoulder was constantly rubbing against his until he finally lifted his arm to rest it behind her on the back of the pew. It was a faintly possessive action that disconcerted Barbara because it appeared to link her with him instead of Todd. Yet Jock rarely looked at her, although she stole several wary glances at his sculpted profile and inadvertently studied the hands that held the hymnbook.

By the time the service was over, her muscles were stiff from being held so tensely. As they filed out of the church, Jock walked with his mother and Barbara finally felt as if she'd been given some breathing room as she left on Todd's arm.

On the way to the car, Lillian asked, "Will you be here for Easter, Todd?"

"I'm afraid not," he answered over his shoulder. "You know that is the hotel's busy time."

"Yes. I thought, perhaps, because of Barbara, you might arrange to have the weekend off," she explained.

"It's a great idea, but it won't work." Todd opened the rear passenger door and helped Barbara into the backseat while Jock assisted his mother into the front passenger seat.

Lillian turned to look at the couple sitting behind her. "Did you know, Barbara, that Florida was named after Easter?"

"No. I was under the impression it was the Spanish word for flower." She frowned at the information with slight astonishment.

"That's partially correct. When Jaun Ponce de Leon landed near St. Augustine, it was Easter, the time of the Feast of Flowers, or Pascua Florida as the Spanish called it."

"How interesting," Barbara murmured as Jock

slid behind the wheel and turned the key in the ignition.

"Speaking of feasts," Todd inserted, "I hope Antonia has dinner ready for us."

"That's another way that you and I differ, Todd," Jock commented. Barbara glanced at the mirror in the center of the windshield and saw the reflection of Jock's eyes, tawny and slumberous like those of a noble beast. Her pulse skittered madly.

"How is that?" Todd asked.

"If I were sitting in the backseat with Barbara, I wouldn't be thinking about food." He shifted the car into gear and let his gaze swing to the front. Barbara went hot all over, remembering vividly the times his lips had devoured hers.

"Jock." The reprimand from Lillian was low and tinged with the embarrassment she felt for Barbara.

"Yes, mother, I'll shut up and be a good boy," he mocked with a cynical, slanting smile.

It was so useless, Barbara thought, averting her gaze to stare out the side window. She didn't have a single defense against his words, let alone a look or his touch. She had won a few minor skirmishes in the past, but the battle for her heart had been lost. Todd's hand closed over hers in silent reassurance. Barbara pushed the realization to the back of her mind, not wanting to make the decision it demanded.

"Swim this afternoon?" Todd suggested.

"All right," Barbara agreed with a nodding shrug of disinterest.

"How about you, J.R.? Want to join us?" he asked.

"Don't issue invitations to me, Todd, or I might take more than you planned. I'll make myself scarce this afternoon. You see, I trust you with Barbara," he told Todd. "But you are a damned fool if you trust her with me. That's a warning, Todd. You'll have to make up your own mind what you're going to do about it . . . if anything."

JOCK KEPT HIS WORD and left the house soon after Sunday dinner. The evening he spent in the den, busy with paperwork. He was absent from the house all day Monday. Although she didn't ask, Barbara guessed he was at the Crosstimber unit of the ranch where they were starting a cattle roundup.

Lillian, Todd and Barbara had gathered on the veranda, minus Jock, for predinner cocktails. As Todd walked to the drink cart to freshen his drink, Lillian glanced at her watch.

"I had better tell Antonia to postpone dinner another twenty minutes. If Jock isn't here by then, we'll eat without him," she sighed. "Excuse me."

"Of course." Barbara smiled absently as the woman moved toward the house doors.

"Would you like some more Coke?" Todd asked. "Or shall I add some rum to it?"

She glanced at her half-empty glass of lime and Coke. For some reason she hadn't wanted any addition of liquor to her drink that evening. A quenched thirst hadn't changed that feeling.

"More Coke only." Barbara handed him the glass to be refilled.

As he poured the soft drink, the ring of the telephone could be heard. Todd paused to listen. It stopped after the second ring and he finished filling her glass, adding a fresh twist of lime to float with the cubes.

"Todd?" Lillian came to the paned doors as he returned the glass to Barbara. "It's long distance for you—your hotel manager. Some problem has come up."

"I'll take it in the den." He walked swiftly toward the door.

Alone, Barbara took her drink and wandered to the edge of the veranda. The slanted rays of the sun glinted off the surface of the swimming pool, while the fanning leaves of the potted palms around the deck swayed in a gentle breeze. Her gaze turned to the lawn, the Spanish oaks and the distant white stables beyond, unconsciously looking for Jock.

He came through the trees with long, slow strides. As her senses were heightened, Barbara felt his tiredness. When he came closer she saw it etched in his face, feathered out from his eyes and drawn around his mouth. Perspiration made the rugged denims and cotton shirt cling to his muscled frame, the material smeared with dirt here and there.

When he saw her, his expression didn't change, nor did his pace. His direction was already carrying him to her and Jock didn't change it. Her blue eyes were hungry for the sight of him and Barbara couldn't take them away from him.

"We were about to give up on you," she said by way of a greeting.

As the distance lessened from feet to inches, she

expected some kind of response from him, one of his usual mocking rejoinders. The last thing she anticipated was the hands that gripped her shoulders and pulled her forward while his mouth descended to seize her lips. Miraculously she avoided spilling the drink in her hand as she reeled under the branding ardor of his kiss. Of its own volition, her body strained closer to his, her back arching. She was engulfed in the heat of his body, overwhelmed by his earthy smell, heightened by perspiration and mingled with horse and leather.

Lingering, Jock mouthed her lips, seizing the lower one between his teeth and lovingly nibbling at it. His hand drifted down to her waist to keep her hips molded to his while his other hand slid up her arm to the drink she held.

"You don't know how many times I've imagined you waiting for me after a long, hard day, with a drink in your hand." Jock lifted his head, taking the glass from her unresisting fingers. "What's this? Rum and Coke? Before she answered, he drank from it. Barbara became momentarily absorbed in the working of his throat as he swallowed and the moisture on his mouth when he took the glass away.

"Just Coke and lime," she told him after he'd already discovered it on his own.

"No rum tonight?" The sheer sexuality of his roaming look had Barbara searching for the breath she lost.

"No, I didn't feel like it." She was suddenly aware of how easily she had let herself be taken into his arms and surrender to the ravaging possession of his kiss. She had not even challenged his right to do it.

"Neither am I," Jock agreed. "I'm not in the mood for forgetting tonight."

As he drained the contents of her glass, Barbara extricated herself from his embrace. His mention of forgetting made her remember his comment about imagining her waiting for him. It irritated her into denouncing it.

"And don't try to fool me with your lies, Jock."

"My lies?" He lifted a bemused brow and walked to the drink cart to refill the glass.

"Yes, your lies," Barbara retorted. "About me waiting for you with a cold drink."

"What makes you think that is a lie?" Jock challenged smoothly, and fixed two glasses instead of one. "I did ask you to come here with me. Or had you forgotten?"

"I hadn't forgotten. I refused to come with you and I've never regretted that decision." She had nearly been crushed when he'd dropped her after a few short days together. She would never have endured the tearing agony if they had spent months together.

The veranda door opened and Todd walked out. "I guess I couldn't expect to have two full weeks without business intruding," he apologized to her.

"Was it serious?" Barbara asked and would have gone to his side except Jock was blocking her way with the fresh glass of lime and Coke.

"The chef walked out and the kitchen is in an uproar. It's nothing new. Claude does this about every two months.'' Todd's attitude dismissed it as a trifling matter. Glancing at Jock, he said, ''We were just about to eat without you.''

''So Barbara mentioned. Is this your drink?'' Jock motioned to the one sitting on the drink cart.

''Yes.'' Todd walked over to get it. ''Had a rough day, did you?''

''A long one,'' Jock conceded. ''Do you and Barbara still want to come over to the Crosstimber unit tomorrow?''

''Sure.'' But he cast a questioning look at Barbara for her affirmation.

''Yes,'' she agreed.

''We'll leave in the morning at eight,'' Jock announced and arched a knowing glance at her. ''Can you get up that early?''

''I can,'' she insisted with an irritated snap.

''Jock, you're home!'' Lillian spotted him the instant she stepped onto the patio. ''I've just had Antonia set dinner back twenty minutes.''

''Good. I'll have time to shower and change first.'' Taking his glass, he started toward the doors. ''If you'll all excuse me.''

''Gladly,'' Lillian laughed. ''You smell like a sweat factory.''

''Be warned,'' Jock said to Todd and Barbara. ''That's what it will be like tomorrow out there.''

''I think we can take it,'' Todd assured him.

''That's right. I'd forgotten. You are going over to watch the roundup tomorrow, aren't you?'' Lillian declared. ''Jock is right. It's a hot, smelly job. But I think you'll find the operation interesting.''

While she was speaking, Jock entered the house. Barbara wasn't certain that it would be wise to see Jock in his environment. It might feed tomorrow's memories. But it was too late. She was committed to go and she didn't want to explain to Todd why she was getting cold feet at the idea.

CHAPTER NINE

A FEW MINUTES after eight o'clock, Barbara walked out of the house with Todd. She started across the courtyard, expecting to see Jock waiting with their horses. Instead a pickup truck and horse trailer were parked in the driveway. Inside the horse van, she could see three saddled horses.

"Aren't we riding the horses there?" she asked Todd.

"No. It's too far. Half the time would be spent riding there. It's easier and quicker to truck the horses where they are needed and ride from that point," he explained.

"I guess I'm forgetting how large this ranch is," Barbara admitted.

When they approached the truck, Jock didn't bother to get out. His arm was resting atop the open window of the truck, his other hand on the steering wheel. His alert gaze ran over Barbara, noting the hat she had borrowed from Lillian.

"Awake?" he asked on a faintly taunting note.

"Wide awake," she insisted.

If she wasn't before, she certainly was now as she realized she would be expected to sit in the middle between the two men. The cab of the pickup was not all that wide. There wasn't a chance she could avoid contact with Jock.

Todd opened the door to the passenger side of the truck and stepped aside for her to climb in. "Would you mind if I sat by the window?" Barbara asked.

"Don't you think it's safe to sit beside me?" Jock taunted before Todd could answer.

"Isn't it safe for me to sit on the outside? Or do you drive so recklessly that the door might pop open and I'll be thrown out?" she countered.

"She has you there, J.R.!" Todd laughed.

"It doesn't matter to me where either one of you sits, but you'd better make up your minds. We aren't going to sit here all day." He turned the ignition key and the engine rumbled to life.

"You can sit by the window and benefit from all the fresh air," Todd volunteered and climbed into the cab, sliding to the middle of the seat.

"Thanks." Barbara hopped in beside him, barely slamming the door shut before Jock put the truck in forward gear.

A ways from the house, Jock turned onto one of the many dirt roads that crisscrossed the ranch, interconnecting the vast sections. Of necessity, he drove at a moderate speed because of the horses in the trailer he pulled behind the truck. The only breeze was generated by the draft the truck made slicing through the still, muggy air. The noise of the engine and the draft blowing in the opened windows of the cab kept conversation at a minimum, and Barbara didn't take part in what there was of it.

Forty minutes from the house, they approached a place where other trucks and trailers were parked on a wide spot in the road. Jock slowed the truck and maneuvered it and the trailer among the others. Despite all the vehicles, there was no one around as Barbara climbed out of the cab, followed by Todd. Beyond the barbed-wire fence and its gate was a long meadow of tall grass, but there wasn't a sign of a horse and rider or a cow.

Barbara walked to the back of the trailer where Jock was unloading the horses. "Where is everyone?"

"Out there." With a nod of his head, he gestured toward the field as he backed the blaze-faced chestnut out of the van, tossing the reins to Barbara. "They've been here since a little after daybreak. We'll catch up with them."

After checking the cinch, Barbara mounted, sitting astride her horse while Todd stepped into the saddle on his bay. Jock was the last to mount after closing the tailgate of the trailer. The big gray horse sidled up to the fence gate and tossed its head eagerly as Jock unlatched the gate and gave it a push. Barbara and Todd rode their horses through and waited until he had shut it.

With an open field before them, the horses needed no second urging to break into a canter. The trucks and trailers soon became distant objects on the horizon, scarcely discernible. It seemed to Barbara that they were shedding the cloak of the present and riding into the past where the creak of saddle leather and the thud of horses' hooves dominated the world.

The land rolled and dipped, undulating like a sea of grass. Here and there, trees poked at the blue sky with a thicker cluster of woods ahead. A distinctive cracking sound could be heard, a sound like a whip. Barbara smiled, guessing they soon would be joining the cowboys, a speculation she wouldn't have been able to make without the information Jock had given her about the bull whips some of the men carried. When Jock angled toward the sound, she knew she was right.

Then Barbara saw them, first the dark hides of bunched cattle followed by three riders. There were thirty or so cows with an apparently equal number of calves. As they rode closer, she noticed the dark blue gray dogs trotting near the cattle, racing up now and then to nip at any that showed an inclination to stray. One rider separated himself from the others and rode out to meet the group.

Jock reined in the gray. "Hello, Clint. How's it going?"

"You know how it is." The big, stocky man shrugged. "With some, it's hide-and-seek. Hello, Todd." He leaned forward to shake hands. "Sorry I missed your party the other night."

"That's all right. It's good to see you again, Clint." Todd smiled and motioned to Barbara. "This is my fiancée, Barbara Haynes. Jock's foreman, Clint Darby."

"I am pleased to meet you, Miss Haynes." He tipped his hat to her, dark hair pressed flat beneath the hatband.

"Same here." She nodded back in acknowledgement.

"Jock tells me you're getting your first look at a roundup," the foreman stated.

"Yes, that's right."

"You'll find most of the excitement is over where Al, Rick, Jessie and Bob are working the trees," he explained and glanced at Jock. "We're moving this bunch to the working pens."

"We'll see you there later on." Jock lifted his hand in a half salute and reined the gray horse away. His backward glance indicated Todd and Barbara were to follow him.

With a wave to the foreman, they turned their horses after the iron-gray horse. Cutting behind the herd, they rode toward the stand of trees growing thickly along the edge of the meadow. Dark outlines of horses and riders moved in a backdrop of dark trunks. The riders were working close to the fence line, driving what animals they found toward the open field.

Most of the cows and their calves moved in the direction the cowboys herded them, but occasionally one would object. Barbara was surprised by the swiftness and agility of the placid-looking animals. The wayward creature would dodge, cut and feint, changing speeds and directions with an ease surprising in an animal of its size and weight. When it was unable to elude the cowboy, it would turn and trot like a plodding elephant.

"We'll keep the cows bunched in the open for the boys," Jock stated.

The cows and calves were already ambling along in the right direction. The sun threw the shade of the trees onto the grass. Walking in their shadows, Barbara soon became aware of the oppressive subtropical climate, the muggy heat baking into her. This far inland, there was no sea breeze from the Atlantic or the Gulf of Mexico, which usually cooled the coastal plains of the peninsular state.

She felt the perspiration gathering between her shoulder blades and under her arms, rivulets running from her collarbone down between her breasts. She longed to trot her horse and stir the air, but she kept it at a walking pace behind the slow-moving cattle, driving them on to a destination only Jock knew. Barbara wiped at the perspiration on her neck and shook it from her fingers.

"It's hot work," commented Jock, observing her action.

"I'm not complaining," she insisted stiffly.

"If it was any hotter out here, you could fry eggs," Todd remarked.

Jock signaled to the riders flushing out the cattle in the trees. Three rode out to take their place, a fourth remaining at his work. With a wave of his hand, Jock motioned for Todd and Barbara to come with him. The chestnut broke into a trot and Barbara felt the blessed stirring of still air.

"Just give your horse its head when you see a cow. It will know what to do," Jock instructed.

Fanning out, the three worked their way among the trees. Jock and the fourth cowboy worked the cows they found. An old black cow appeared to submit to Jock's herding into the open without complaint. The instant it was past Barbara, it whirled on a dime and attempted to race through the riders back to the trees. The chestnut pivoted to give chase with no command from Barbara. She kept her balance, gripping the saddle horn and hugging her legs tight to the stirrup leather.

When the agile horse blocked it from slipping through, the cow changed direction and raced for the open field. Barbara raced after it, hearing the thudding of galloping hooves following her. She spared a lightning glance over her shoulder to see Jock in pursuit of the cow, as well, the big gray horse seeming to be stretched out flat.

In the open meadow, the cow began a wide circle to get back to the trees. The air whipped at Barbara's face, billowing her blouse behind her. She didn't take her eyes from the cow's black hide, trusting her horse to avoid any holes or ruts in the thick grass. When she turned the cow away from the trees, there was a wild, exhilarating feeling of success. Jock was at her side to keep it heading in the right direction. When the cow broke into a run, it was to join the small bunch.

Slowing the chestnut, Barbara leaned forward to pat its sweating neck. The wild ride had left her breathless and elated. She laughed from the sheer stimulation of the experience.

"That was exciting!" Her eyes sparkled and danced with brilliant blue lights.

"You have the makings of a real cow hunter if you stay around awhile longer." The flashing white of his smile was warm and vital, sharing her enthusiasm for the ride and unmarred by cynicism or mockery.

Danger signals went off. Jock's potent charm tugged painfully at her heartstrings. But she had danced to its tune before and paid the price. She resisted its magnetic pull, turning away, her own smile fading into nothing.

"But I'm not staying longer. Todd and I are leaving at the end of the week." Barbara deliberately coupled her name with Todd's in her reminder.

His hand reached out to grip the reins ahead of her hold and check her mount. "You won't admit it yet, will you?" Jock demanded stiffly. "You still won't see that Todd isn't for you."

"No, I don't see that," she retorted. "But even if he isn't, I'm sure about one thing—neither are you!" She jammed her heels into the chestnut's sides and sent it leaping free of Jock's restraining grip.

Once loose, Barbara didn't attempt to outrace the superior speed of the gray horse, but slowed her mount to a sedate canter. She rode toward the trees to rejoin Todd. When Jock drew alongside, she didn't alter her course and he didn't attempt to sidetrack her.

"Still all in one piece after that hair-raising ride?" Todd joked when she reined in beside him, seeking the protection of his company.

"Where were you? Barbara forced a casual smile on her face. "I thought you'd come, too."

"Are you kidding?" he laughed. "You can go racing at that breakneck speed, but I know my limitations."

"It was fun." Because it *had* been, even if the confrontation with Jock had not been.

"But it isn't my kind of fun," Todd replied without apology and smiled.

After combing that section of fence line and woods, they had banded together a small herd of cows and calves. They drove them to the working pens, near the road where all the trucks and trailers were parked. They arrived at the noontime break.

Going home for lunch was impractical for the cowboys, considering the distances involved on the ranch. A meal of hot stew and sandwiches was served out of the back of a pickup truck along with gallons of black coffee. There was also an insulated cask of drinking water.

"Drink plenty of water," Jock advised, "to replace what you lost out there in the sun." His gaze raked Barbara, noting the way perspiration had plastered her blouse to her curves. "Even though coffee is liquid, it isn't as effective as plain water."

Unnerved by his penetrating look, her reply was cool. Even without his advice, Barbara wouldn't have visited the water keg to slake her parched throat in a hurry. She said as much, but his comment did remind her that the possibility of heatstroke was not something to dismiss lightly. So she drank plenty of water as she had been ordered.

Todd picked out a place in the shade where they could eat their lunch. Jock didn't join them, having his meal with the men. It was a scene permeated with the noise of bawling calves and male voices, and the smell of animal sweat and another faintly obnoxious odor.

Finished with his meal, Todd leaned against a tree

trunk with a contented sigh. Barbara removed her hat and ran her fingers through her long black curls to let the air reach her damp scalp. She glanced at the group of cowboys, standing around drinking coffee before returning to their work.

Jock was among them, standing tall and wide legged. He easily stood out in the group of men, although he dressed no different from them. It had always been that way, but Barbara had assumed it was his striking male looks. Studying him, she realized it was his easy air of command: authority was bred into every bone. His very air demanded notice. He didn't have to shout to make himself heard. People automatically listened when he spoke.

"This is J.R.'s milieu; it's his bailiwick, not mine," Todd remarked. "It's a good thing this ranch is his. All this rugged outdoor life isn't for me. Give me silks and satins and diamonds anytime. What about you?" His gaze slid with absent curiosity to Barbara.

"Diamonds and furs aren't exactly my line. My needs are much simpler, but I like my comfort," she admitted. "So does Jock," she added unconsciously.

"Yes, but he's in his element here."

Barbara couldn't have agreed more. Jock embraced the challenge of running this vast holding, of dealing with the vagaries of nature and its whims. While Todd's position as hotel owner was comparable in power and prestige to Jock's, he didn't have to combat disease, drought and the land.

Trying to compare the two brothers was impossible. An apple couldn't be likened to an orange, even though they were both fruit. In the final analysis it came down to personal preference. Barbara sighed and drank more water. It was probably just as well there weren't many similarities between them. She wouldn't want to look at Todd and imagine Jock.

The groaning creak of saddle leather signaled that the men were riding out. Barbara looked up as Jock approached their shaded spot. The touch of his gold brown eyes had her stomach muscles tensing.

"Do you want a closer look at the operation from this end, after the cows have been rounded up?" He directed his question at her.

Barbara realized that Todd was probably familiar with all of this. "Yes, I would like that." Picking up her hat, she pushed to her feet and glanced at Todd, expecting him to do the same.

Instead, he settled more comfortably in his position against the tree. "You go ahead. What breeze we have is blowing away from me toward the pens. I'd just as soon leave the stench over there," he smiled.

"Ready?" Jock prompted.

Barbara hesitated, but she could hardly refuse to go with him now. Besides, she was interested in seeing it even if Todd wasn't.

"Sure," she agreed and started forward, carrying her hat.

Jock matched his stride with the length of hers to walk at her side as they crossed the grassy space to the iron pens of metal pipe. Activity had already begun inside it, animals milling as a horse and rider entered their midst, cowboys moving about within the confines and outside of it. Barbara paused at the horizontal bars.

"Once they are inside the working pens, we separate the calves from the cows," Jock explained.

It wasn't a situation that pleased either the cow or the calf. The horse and rider didn't give either an option and Barbara was reminded of the cutting-horse competition she had watched at the arena. There, it had been an exhibition of skill. Here, that skill was being put to practical use as the calves were cut out and herded into a narrow corral. The bawling cries of the confused and frightened calves were answered by the frantic lowing of their mothers.

"From the calf corral—" Jock walked toward it and Barbara followed him "—the calves are put into that chute one at a time. The chute is called a 'turnover' for the obvious reason that once a calf is locked inside, the chute 'turns over' to make an operating table." Barbara watched the procedure as he explained it. "The calf is inoculated, dehorned with those pinchers and receives an identifying earmark; the bull calves are castrated, and all are branded."

The branding iron was typical of the ones she'd seen in Western movies. In this case, there was a scrolled S at the end of the iron rod, the Sandoval brand she had noticed on the hips of the cows. Instead of the traditional campfire heating the iron to a red-hot color, a butane torch was used. She heard the iron sizzle as it was pushed on the calf's hip and smelled the acrid stench of burning hair and hide.

She half turned away from the unpleasant smell. Once branded, the calf was released to return to its mother and the next calf was loaded into the chute.

"With the turnover we can handle an average of fifty calves an hour. When we had to rope them and stretch them out on the ground, we were lucky to do that many in half a day. Thanks to the chute, it's a smooth, efficient operation with less wear and tear on the calves and the men. It's known as progress—" his gaze rested on her face and his voice lowered in volume and tone "—which is something you and I aren't making."

Barbara stiffened at the unexpected injection of a personal reference. "We aren't making any progress because I'm engaged to Todd," she flashed in defiance and continued to stare at the calf corral.

"You aren't in love with him," Jock accused. The butt of a rawhide whip was laid against her cheek to turn her to face him. "You couldn't be in love with him and respond the way you do to me. And you do respond, Barbara. I know the way your pulse beats so rapidly in your throat when I kiss you . . . the same way it's doing now." His gaze flicked pointedly to the hollow of her throat. "I've heard the kitten sighs you make in your throat when I'm loving you, sounds I don't think you are even aware you make. But you do. It's useless to deny it."

"I don't deny it." How could she? But Barbara managed to keep the rising tide of emotion in check, despite the subtle seductive quality in his voice. "Sex was always good between us. But you are a master at arousing a woman to her fullest desires.

Don't pretend that I'm the first woman who has responded so completely to you. Your technique is excellent.''

Her reply made him impatient. She could see it in the thinning line of his mouth. Jock wasn't touching her, except with that rawhide-wrapped handle of the whip, but he stood so close she could feel his body heat.

"I never implied that you were the first or only woman I had made love to," he said thinly.

That stabbed. She was just one of many, part of his stable he kept around for his amusement. But she wasn't going to be available to him every time he snapped his fingers.

"When we split up, you suggested that we might become friends. At the time, I refused because I didn't have any intention of ever seeing you again," Barbara declared in a taut, strained voice. "But since I'm marrying your brother, it might be the practical solution. It was your idea. Maybe you should consider it again."

Turning on her heel, she walked away from him. She had taken less than a half a dozen steps when something made a swooshing sound in the air near her and a strap began wrapping itself around her waist. It took a second to realize it was his whip coiling around her with hardly a sting to its touch.

With it wrapped tightly around her waist, Jock yanked her toward him while walking to meet her, not allowing any slack in the whip. She could see the anger flaming in his brown eyes, but she was angry, too.

"You enjoy making a scene, don't you?" Barbara flared.

"Don't walk away from me, Barbara," he threatened in a savage underbreath. "Don't ever walk away from me again."

"Or else what, Jock?" she taunted him. "What will you do?"

His hard features were almost hauntingly grim. "Don't push me, woman," Jock warned huskily and released the tension on the whip so that it fell loose from her waist.

There was a rawness to his look that made Barbara turn away. Jock didn't try to stop her this time when she started toward the tree Todd was sitting beneath. He had dozed off, wakening when she slumped to the ground beside him. Barbara began to think Todd was like the three monkeys. He never seemed to see, hear or say anything wrong.

Todd noted her pale face and commented, "The smell of those pens gets to you, doesn't it? Now you know why I didn't go over there."

"Yes," she murmured.

"Want to ride? Get some fresh air after all that stench of burning hide?" He straightened from the tree, flexing his shoulders.

"Why not?" Barbara shrugged, not wanting to stay in Jock's vicinity.

It was late afternoon before Jock found them and suggested they should load the horses up to start for the house. As they rode to the horse trailer, his eyes kept seeking hers, but Barbara avoided them. For some reason she felt very vulnerable and didn't know why. Again she sat on the outside by the window, using Todd as a buffer and keeping out of the conversation.

CHAPTER TEN

BARBARA LAY IN HER BED, unable to sleep. After the previous day's riding and the restless night before, she had expected to tumble into an exhausted sleep tonight. Instead, her thoughts kept twisting and turning in her mind, chasing away sleep.

Rolling over, she looked at her watch on the bedside table. In the dim moonlight glowing through the balcony doors, she saw it was after midnight. Giving up, Barbara tossed the bed covers aside and climbed out of the bed. The softness of the night called her to the balcony.

The air was warm and languid so Barbara didn't bother with the robe lying on the foot of her bed. She pushed open the doors to her private balcony and stepped outside. A crescent moon seemed to look down on her with a half-closed sleepy eye. Barbara sighed in envy and wandered to the iron-lace railing.

Stars littered the velvet black sky and a faint breeze whispered in the moss-draped trees. The balcony overlooked the rear lawn on the opposite side of the house from the veranda. A night bird sang somewhere in the trees and Barbara unconsciously searched for the feathered creature sharing the night with her.

She leaned over the iron railing, staring at the thick branches. Her side vision caught a flicker of movement in the trees, but when she tried to focus on it, she saw nothing. It was so dark within the shadows of those trees that it was unlikely she could distinguish any shape.

Barbara didn't hear the bird again and guessed it had flown away. She wished she could fly away with it, soar into the cloudless sky and lose herself in the shimmer of stars.

Straightening, she wandered along the balcony's edge, trailing a hand along the railing, around an arching pillar onto the railing again stopping at the corner. Half sitting on the narrow iron rail, she leaned a shoulder against a concrete arch and let the peaceful serenity of the night soothe her troubled mind.

Once, Barbara thought she heard a movement inside the house, but all the rooms were dark, except for the small lamp by her bed. She dismissed the sound as the natural groaning of the house.

After a while she drifted into a night dream of abstract things, the immensity of the universe and the minuscule importance of one person on the planet. Far off came a sound that should have been familiar to her, but her concentration didn't permit it to register.

The sound of a footfall on the balcony did. Barbara straightened in alarm at the dark figure of the intruder, her heart leaping into her throat. It beat all the more wildly when she recognized Jock.

"How did you get out here?" she demanded in shock. "Why are you here?"

"I saw the light on. I knocked at the door. When you didn't answer, I came in to make sure you were all right," Jock explained, moving toward her in a leisurely stroll.

Barbara turned back to the night, gripping the railing with both her hands. "I'm all right, so you can leave."

"Couldn't sleep?" he questioned and stopped when he was less than two feet from her.

"No." Surely it was obvious, her impatient tone said.

"Neither could I." Jock paused, but she didn't offer a reply. "The truth is I didn't see your light on. I was out walking and saw you on the balcony. Unfortunately there aren't any trellises or vines to climb so I had to use the more conventional approach of the stairs."

"Why bother? I don't want your company," Barbara retorted, her heart telling her that was a lie.

"Don't you?" He let his hand glide over her shoulder, bared by the slender strap of her pajama top.

With a shrug Barbara eluded his caressing touch, frantically wishing for the robe she had left on the bed. The moon and starlight had silvered her skin. The lateness of the hour became much too evocative.

"Will you please leave?" she hissed desperately.

"What if someone wakes up and finds you in my bedroom at this hour?"

"With your sexy pajamas on and the bed all rumpled." Jock carried the thought a step further. "Don't worry. Everyone is sound asleep except us. They aren't likely to wake up unless you make a lot of noise."

"If you don't leave, I'll start screaming," she threatened.

"No, you won't," he chuckled softly. "You don't want my mother or Todd to find me in here 'at this hour,'" He stressed the phrase with mocking emphasis. "Why do you suppose you and I are the only ones who can't sleep?"

"I really don't know and I don't care." Barbara tried to sound emphatic, but his voice was so velvety that it took the starch out of her reply.

"Do you think it might be this soft, southern night?" Jock mused.

This time when his hands touched her, they curved onto both her shoulders. Barbara was trapped—on one side by the railing, on a second by the corner of the balcony, and on the other two sides Jock could easily block her way.

"Jock, leave me alone...please." It was a whispered plea while her body quivered in uncontrollable reaction to the caress of his hands.

"That isn't what you want." His head bent to her neck, his mouth trailing a lazy fire along the nape. "You want the same thing I do, honey. Why keep fighting it?"

"Don't." Barbara tipped her head back to stop the

dangerously sensual teasing of his mouth on her skin.

Jock simply transferred his attentions to the exposed curve of her neck and shoulder while his hands slid down her rib cage to cross in front of her stomach. A pervading warmth spread through her limbs as he pulled her back against his hard length. Her shoulders, spine and hips were pressed firmly along his male contours.

Cupping a hipbone in one hand, Jock slid his other hand beneath the lace pajama top to seek the ripe fullness of a breast. The male outline of his aroused need was imprinted on her hips, kindling an answering ache within her.

"Todd isn't the man for you," Jock murmured into her ear, sending goose bumps of wild ecstasy over her flesh. "Why won't you admit it? You want me to make love to you as much as I want to."

Barbara fought the insidious weakness ravaging her senses in the only way she could find. "If that isn't an example of a macho male mentality, nothing is." Her disturbed voice was laced with sarcasm. "You think all you have to do is hold your body against mine and I'll agree to anything."

"Won't you?" he mocked confidently.

To prove his point, his fingers teased the peak of her breast while the hand on her hipbone moved to make slow, sensuous forays over her stomach, igniting fires in its pit. Giving in for a glorious second, Barbara relaxed against him. Jock half turned to let the corner pillar of the balcony support him. When she made a move to pivot toward him, his arms loosened to permit it.

Barbara took the opportunity to twist out of his embrace. Jock started to straighten, then waited as her weak legs could take her no farther away from him than just out of arm's length.

"Come here, honey," he invited.

"Why won't you leave me alone?" Barbara protested in a husky dry voice.

"I'm not leaving you alone until you take that ring off your finger." He pushed from the pillar to claim her.

In agitation, Barbara spun away and half ran to the glass-paned doors leading to her bedroom. She yanked at the diamond on her finger, finally pulling it free. By then she was inside the bedroom and Jock was behind her.

"There! It's off!" She slapped it on the bedside table within the circle of the lamplight so he could see the light reflected on the many-faceted stone.

"That's where it belongs." Smiling lazily, he came toward her and reached out to take her shoulders. "And this is where you belong." He curved her trembling body inside the circle of his arms.

Her soft curves fitted themselves to his male shape with familiar ease, and they were welded by their combined body heat. Before she could escape it, his mouth covered hers in a long, drugging kiss. Her fingers curled into the material of his shirt sleeves as she clung tenaciously to an invisible link with sanity.

When he let her up for air, Barbara seized on that

link. "I took the ring off. You said you'd leave me alone if I did," she reminded him in a fierce, breathless voice.

Jock lifted his head to gaze at her with an incredulous and angry frown. "You don't mean it? You can't expect me to leave you alone now?"

"I'm not wearing Todd's engagement ring. I promise I won't put it back on when you go." She strained against his hold, bending her head to avoid his eyes. "You promised, Jock. Don't you mean what you say?"

He grabbed a handful of black hair to force her head back. "You don't want me to leave. Your lips tell me one thing, but your body tells me something different. I know its needs as well as I know my own. And you want me to make love to you," he insisted.

"I want you to go," Barbara declared on a choked sob. "You said you would."

His hands slipped to her shoulders, fingers digging into the bare flesh. "What are you trying to do to me?" Jock demanded harshly.

"I'm trying to make you do what you said. There isn't any ring on my finger. Now leave me alone!" Her voice broke on the last.

Her anguished blue eyes watched the indecision warring in his expression. Barbara knew if Jock persisted, she couldn't deny him. At last he pushed her away from him and she stumbled backward onto the bed.

"I'll leave. This time, I'll leave," he agreed angrily. "But it isn't what you really want and you'll never make me believe otherwise."

"Then go." She was losing her control. She could feel the sobs building like a volcano before an eruption. She didn't know how much longer she could hold back the torrent of tears.

"Thanks to you, we are both going to spend a frustrated, miserable night alone when we could have had the satisfaction of each other," he growled.

When he continued to stand in the same place, Barbara challenged in desperation, "Are you going to leave or not?"

"I'm going!" Jock strode to the door, yanking it open. He paused to look back at her. "Have a rotten night!" And he slammed the door shut with a vengeance.

The dam burst and Barbara grabbed for the pillow to smother her sobs. She had sworn she would never cry over Jock again, but she was. There wasn't anything she could do to stop it.

Minutes couldn't measure the time she cried. When the sobbing finally subsided, she ached all over. She lay there hurting with a pain that was physical and mental.

Barbara didn't know how long she lay there staring at the shadows on the ceiling. Sleep wouldn't come to ease her torment. Turning her head on the pillow, she glanced at the bedside table. Todd's engagement ring glittered in the pool of light. Jock had forced her to make one right decision. She wasn't going to marry Todd. Jock would always stand in the way of whatever happiness Todd might have been able to give her.

Barbara realized the affection she had felt for Todd had never truly been the right kind. She had needed him so desperately as a friend that she had taken his ring, but for that same reason she had never been able to accept him as a lover. It would probably be a very long time before she could ever accept any man in that role—because of Jock. He had taken so much from her that she had little left to give.

There was no reason to continue the farce of an engagement. She would return the diamond to Todd in the morning—which couldn't be more than a couple of hours away. Barbara rolled back to stare at the ceiling again. She faced another realization. There was no more reason to linger here at the ranch. Remaining in Jock's company was inviting disaster. She couldn't risk it.

A second time, she crawled out of bed. This time it was to drag her suitcases out of the closet and begin emptying drawers and hangers to pack her clothes. She wasn't going to let anyone talk her out of it—not anyone . . . and especially not Jock.

FROM HER BALCONY Barbara watched the sun rise. She heard Jock go downstairs; she recognized his firm tread on the stairs. A little while later Barbara heard Lillian stirring, then the shower running in the room next to hers—Todd's room. At about the same time that she heard Todd leave his room, she saw Jock walking toward the stables. It was the last time she would see him. Barbara knew this image of him would be forever branded on her memory. She watched until Jock was out of sight, then left the balcony.

Her suitcases were stacked neatly by the door. She paused to pick up the engagement ring from the bedside table and continued to the hall. Todd was halfway down the stairs when she started down.

"Todd!" she called to him to wait.

"You're up early this morning," he commented, stopping in the foyer. His brown eyes surveyed the blue flowered skirt and matching solid blue blouse, a bow sash at the throat. "You are really dressed up this morning. Are you planning on going somewhere?"

"Yes." Barbara halted on the last step to look at him, wondering where to begin.

"Hey?" Todd frowned, his hand reaching out to trace her cheekbone. "Where did those circles under your eyes come from? Didn't you sleep last night?"

"Not much," she admitted. "Here." She pressed the engagement ring in the palm of his hand and closed his fingers over it.

"What's this?" He glanced down at the ring, his frown deepening.

"I can't marry you, Todd. I realized that last night. So I'm giving your ring back to you," Barbara explained in a stilted voice.

"Is this what kept you up all night?" he questioned.

"Partly. I'm sorry, Todd," she apologized with genuine sincerity. "I should never have taken your ring in the first place. And I shouldn't have let you talk me into keeping it when I found out Jock was your brother.''

"It doesn't matter about J.R.," he protested. "I wanted you to have it because I loved you.''

"I never meant to hurt you, Todd. Please believe that. You've been so good to me that I wish things were different.'' Her blue eyes were wide and troubled, asking him to understand. "I know what it's like and I don't want to hurt you.''

Todd took a deep breath and rolled the ring in his palm, studying it for a few silent seconds. "What you are trying to say, very gently, is that you don't love me, isn't it?''

"Not the way I should. Not the way you deserve,'' Barbara admitted. "I'm sorry.''

"It's still J.R., isn't it? You're still in love with him,'' he guessed. The corners of his mouth were pulled down with a grim wryness.

"I didn't want it to be that way.''

"I can't really say that I'm surprised.'' Todd's glance was resigned. "I think I suspected it was going to turn out like this when you told me who J.R. really was.''

"I wish we had both known before we came here.''

"Don't look so glum.'' He curved an arm around her shoulder and brought her down the last step. "If we had known, we wouldn't have come and we would have always wondered whether you were really over him. Now we know definitely that you aren't.'' Todd looked at the ring one last time before he slipped it into his pocket. "Does J.R. know about this? That you are giving back the ring?"

"Yes," she whispered, nodding. It was a comforting arm that was around her. Right now, she needed Todd's undemanding solace although she would no longer lean on it as she had done in the past. "It doesn't change anything with Jock," Barbara clarified that point quickly.

"So what comes next?"

"I want to leave, Todd—today—this morning." With each pause, she went a step further in stating her objective.

He held her away from his side to look at her. "But you don't have to be at work until Monday. You still have four days left of your vacation. There's no reason for you to go back yet."

"Yes, there is," Barbara insisted. "We aren't engaged anymore, Todd. I can't stay here under false pretenses."

"You're my guest," he pointed out. "A friend instead of a fiancée."

"I can't stay here, Todd. Not with Jock here." She finally offered the real reason.

"No, I suppose not," he sighed.

"Just because I want to go back is no reason for you to cut your vacation short. If you drive me into town, I can catch a bus," Barbara offered.

"No bus. I brought you here. I'll take you back," Todd promised.

"All my luggage is packed. I have it sitting in my room by the door," she explained.

"You really are determined to leave this morning, aren't you?" he laughed. "What did you do? Stay up all night packing once you'd made up your mind?"

"Yes," Barbara admitted, his laughter drawing a faint smile.

"If I hadn't agreed to take you—or drive you into town, you would have walked, wouldn't you?" he accused.

"Yes. The sooner I get away from here, the better off I'll be," she declared.

Todd studied her thoughtfully. "Aren't you going to tell J.R. goodbye? Does he know you are leaving?"

"No. And I don't want to see him. We said our goodbyes six months ago. I don't want to go through it again." A cold chill quivered through her shoulders and Todd pulled her close to his side, rubbing her arm as if to warm her.

"I won't try to change your mind. If you don't want to see him before you go, I'm not going to argue. But knowing my brother, he isn't going to be too happy about it when he finds out," he said.

"It doesn't matter whether he likes it or not. That's the way it's going to be," Barbara stated decisively, more so than she felt.

"There is one thing I want clear between us. I know we aren't engaged anymore, but I'd like to go on seeing you occasionally." He gave her a wry smile, reading her thoughts. "I'm not going to try to put the ring back on your finger. It's just that I like being with you and I wouldn't want that to stop because of this."

"When I get back to Miami—" Barbara paused, taking her time to finish the difficult sentence "—I'm going to ask the airline for a transfer."

"Where?" Todd frowned.

"I don't care, just as long as it's far away from Florida," she added tightly.

"No, I'm not going to sit quietly by while you do that." Todd shook his head. "I don't like the idea of your being alone, Barbara."

"Don't you see, Todd," Barbara reasoned, "the last time you helped me through this. You taught me I could make it. This time I have to do it on my own. I can't lean on you forever.

"Maybe not, but—" He stopped whatever his next argument was going to be and smiled. "We'll talk about this later. I'll get your luggage out to the car while you pour us some coffee and juice."

"Yes, and I want to say goodbye to your mother . . . and explain," she agreed.

"You do that." Todd kissed her on the cheek, his lips lingering a little longer than necessary before he let her go to climb the stairs.

Barbara watched him take the first flight and remembered what Jock had said. Todd would get over losing her. He always had enough love left for the next person. She should take lessons from him in how that's done, she thought as she turned from the stairs.

Crossing through the living room, she entered the dining room. Lillian Gaynor was seated at the table, sipping at her morning coffee. She smiled in surprise when Barbara walked in.

"My, but you are up early this morning," Lillian declared.

Was it that much of a rarity that everyone commented on it, Barbara wondered. She hadn't thought she had slept very late while she was there.

"Yes, I am." Barbara glanced at her watch, noticing for the first time that it was a little before seven, which was early for her.

"Coffee? You look very nice this morning. Are you and Todd going somewhere?" She asked the questions while she offered Barbara a cup of coffee.

"Actually . . . Todd is driving me back to Miami. I'm leaving this morning," Barbara announced.

"So soon?" Lillian stopped in the act of filling a cup. "I thought you were staying until this weekend?"

"There has been a change in plans. You see, I've returned Todd's engagement ring." She met the older woman's look and tried to appear more calm and in total control than she felt.

"When did this happen?" Lillian was still trying to take it all in.

"This morning. I talked to Todd just a few minutes ago," Barbara explained.

"Where is he?" Lillian glanced toward the archway.

"He's putting my luggage in the car."

"What did Jock have to say?" To herself, she added, *no wonder he left the house in such a temper this morning*.

"Nothing. He doesn't know I'm leaving," Barbara admitted and took the cup from the woman to sip at its hot contents.

"He doesn't know?" Lillian repeated. "Aren't you going to tell him goodbye?"

"No. I don't see any point," she answered, shrugging.

"But surely—"

"I have chosen neither of your sons. They both know it," Barbara replied. Jock just didn't happen to fully believe it, and she didn't want to get caught in the trap of trying to convince him. "Todd asked me to have some coffee and juice ready for him."

Lillian began pouring another cup. "You are leaving right away?"

"Yes. It will be more comfortable driving if we go before the sun is too hot." She pretended that was the reason.

Todd came striding into the dining room, brushing his hands in a gesture of finished work. "That didn't take long. Is that my coffee?" He glanced at the cup his mother was filling.

"Yes. Barbara has just told me she's leaving. You surely weren't planning to leave without something to eat?" Lillian protested.

"We'll catch a bite along the way," Todd shrugged.

"Nonsense!" Lillian dismissed that immediately. "There are some Danish pastries in the kitchen. You are at least going to eat that before you leave."

"I'm not really hungry," Barbara protested.

"It doesn't pay to argue with her," Todd inserted.

"She'll get her own way. She always does."

"Todd is right," Lillian agreed with him.

"Go get the pastries, mother," he ordered.

"I won't be a minute," she promised and rose from the table to go to the kitchen.

"Pour me some orange juice, will you, Barbara?" Todd requested.

She poured him a glass and one for herself. It had seemed churlish to argue about the sweet rolls, but she disliked even that small delay. Sitting in the chair next to Todd's, she set his glass in front of him and drank from hers.

CHAPTER ELEVEN

AT LILLIAN'S INSISTENCE, Barbara double-checked her room to be certain she hadn't left any of her belongings behind. There was nothing in the room that belonged to her, except some memories that she knew would follow.

Todd and his mother were waiting in the foyer as she descended the steps. Barbara felt awkward when the older woman came forward to hug her goodbye. There was apprehension in Lillian's brown eyes when she stepped back.

"Goodbye, dear. I would have liked to have you for a daughter-in-law," she said.

"Goodbye, Lillian." Barbara didn't return the comment by saying she would have liked Lillian as her mother-in-law, because it was all academic at this point.

"Ready?" Todd opened one of the double doors for her. "I'll be back sometime late this afternoon, mother."

"All right."

Barbara paused in the courtyard to look back and wave a hand to the woman before Todd stepped out and closed the door. He walked to her side. Guilt made her say again, "You don't have to drive me back, Todd."

He took her arm as they passed the fountain in the courtyard. The sound of the falling water reminded Barbara of tears. Todd's car was parked in front. He reached ahead of her to open the passenger door.

"What's this message all about, Todd?" Jock's voice demanded.

Barbara whirled to see him stalking from the veranda through the courtyard toward them. Her gaze jerked back at Todd to accuse him, *how could you?* Her mind had already leaped to the conclusion that Todd had let his brother know she was leaving.

"Antonia came to the stable with some garbled message from mother that Barbara was leaving," Jock continued, evidently not seeing her standing on the other side of the car door until he had emerged from the courtyard.

Lillian had sent the message, not Todd. Barbara realized she should have known better. Either way the damage was done. Jock's piercing eyes were narrowing on her as awareness sunk in like an angry thundercloud that the message hadn't been garbled.

"It's true," Barbara confirmed. "I am leaving."

"Without letting me know? Without even a goodbye?" he accused.

"How many times do we have to say it?" she countered. His gaze sliced to her left hand. "I gave the ring back to Todd. I told you I was going to."

"You've told me a lot of things, and your actions have told me a lot more. You aren't leaving, Barbara," Jock stated.

"Leave me alone, Jock. Just let me go!" She turned to slide onto the car seat.

"Not this time." His hand seized her arm in a punishing grip. "I'm not letting you go. We're going to talk this out."

"No." Barbara strained against his grip and appealed to Todd. "Todd, I want to leave."

"You aren't going anywhere unless I say so." Jock didn't give his brother a chance to reply. "Todd knows that one word from me and every exit from this ranch will have a man posted at the gate within minutes. You couldn't leave Sandoval land without being stopped. You are going to talk to me."

"He's right, Barbara," Todd offered quietly.

She flashed Jock a mutinous look to conceal the pain inside. "It looks as if I don't have any choice."

"You don't."

His sun-browned features were set in hard lines as he pulled her away from the car and pushed her ahead of him toward the house. This was a confrontation Barbara hadn't wanted and she took advantage of these few minutes without conversation to prepare her defenses, meager as they were. In the house Jock directed her to the small, wood-paneled den and closed the door.

"Why are you leaving?" he demanded, squaring her around so she faced him. His hands were hard on her shoulders.

"Because there isn't any reason to stay," she retorted stiffly, keeping the inner tremors out of her voice.

"I want you to stay. Isn't that a reason?"

"Not a good enough one." Her gaze wavered under the blazing force of his.

The answer earned her a hard shake. "Not good enough, is it? You've got me half out of my mind and it isn't good enough," Jock muttered savagely. "Haven't I made it obvious how much I want you? I've done nothing but think about you day and night—"

"Stop it!" She cut across his words with an angry protest. "Six months, Jock! You never gave me a thought for six months! I didn't get so much as a telephone call or a postcard from you! Don't try to make me believe that you were all tied up in knots all this time! You never even tried to reach me!"

"No, I didn't!" he shouted. "I'm not in the habit of going begging to a woman to ask her to love me."

"I'm sure you don't have to. You can get all the women you want with a snap of your fingers, so leave me alone!" Barbara cried in agitation.

"But I want you!"

"To be what? Your friend? Or your lover?" She hurled at him the words that had wounded her so deeply. "You can't make up your mind, can you? If I stay, how long will it be before you suggest we be friends again? Three days? Four?"

"Friends?" Jock frowned. "You're damned right I want you to be my friend. I want a wife that is more than a lover. I want someone who will be at my side, not just in my bed!"

The one single word stole all of Barbara's hurt anger. It seemed like a shining light, flickering uncertainly to guide her through the darkness. She stared at him, fearful—hopeful.

"Your wife?" she repeated in a breathy murmur.

"Yes, my wife," Jock snapped.

"You . . . never said anything about that before," Barbara whispered, waiting for him to blow out the light that was burning brighter with each second.

"I didn't?" The hardness began leaving his chiseled features. "I took it for granted—"

With a sobbing cry of joy, Barbara wrapped her arms around him to hug him tightly. She bit at her lip, wanting to laugh and cry at the same time and unwilling to do either as she cherished this moment.

"Honey?" He cupped her face in his hands and lifted it so he could see the happiness brimming in her eyes. "What did you think I was proposing? I love you. Of course I want you to be my wife."

"Of course, he says." Laughter bubbled in her throat. "When you asked me to come with you to the ranch and I refused, I thought you just wanted me for my . . . loving companionship."

"I wanted you to meet my mother, to see our home, where our children will live, and the ranch. I wanted us to have some time to get to know each other," Jock explained in a husky voice. "You have to admit the few short days we were together, we crammed in a lot of loving and little else."

"And I thought you were only offering me an illicit relationship," she breathed. "And I nearly accepted. I would have if you had asked me again, because I loved you so much I didn't care."

"Imagine how I felt when I suggested we get acquainted and you told me, in no uncertain terms, that you didn't want to get better acquainted with me?" Jock countered, able to smile at the thought now. "Here was the woman I wanted for my wife—and all she wanted was a carefree weekend in bed with no strings. She didn't sound like a likely candidate for motherhood, not of my children."

"When you suggested we be friends instead of lovers, I thought you were letting me down easy—that you were tired of me."

"Tired of you? That will be the day!" Bending his head, he found her mouth and kissed her with a deep hunger that had her heart spinning.